Born on
a Tuesday

Born on a Tuesday

A Novel

Elnathan John

Black Cat
New York

A version of the chapter "Bayan Layi" first appeared in Per Contra, issue 25.
Published in Nigeria in 2015 by Cassava Republic Press.

Published simultaneously in Canada
Printed in the United States of America

FIRST EDITION

ISBN 978-0-8021-2482-1
eISBN 978-0-8021-8990-5

Black Cat
an imprint of Grove Atlantic
154 West 14th Street
New York, NY 10011

Distributed by Publishers Group West

groveatlantic.com

16 17 18 19   10 9 8 7 6 5 4 3 2 1

For the boys who will never be known
And the girls who become numbers—
Stars without a name

A Star without a Name

When a baby is taken from the wet nurse,
it easily forgets her
and starts eating solid food.
Seeds feed a while on ground,
then lift up into the sun.
So you should taste the filtered light
and work your way toward wisdom
with no personal covering.
That's how you came here, like a star
without a name. Move across the night sky
with those anonymous lights.

—Rumi

PART ONE

Bayan Layi

2003

The boys who sleep under the kuka tree in Bayan Layi like to boast about the people they have killed. I never join in because I have never killed a man. Banda has, but he doesn't like to talk about it. He just smokes wee-wee while they talk over each other's heads. Gobedanisa's voice is always the loudest. He likes to remind everyone of the day he strangled a man. I never interrupt his story even though I was there with him and saw what happened. Gobedanisa and I had gone into a lambu to steal sweet potatoes but the farmer had surprised us while we were there. As he chased us, swearing to kill us if he caught us, he fell into a bush trap for antelopes. Gobedanisa did not touch him. We just stood by and watched as he struggled and struggled and then stopped struggling.

I don't care that Gobedanisa lies about it but sometimes I just want to ask him to shut up. The way he talks about killing, you would think he would get aljanna for it, that Allah would reserve the best spot for him. I know why he talks like that. He tells it to keep the smaller boys in awe of him. And to make them fear him. His face is a map of scars, the most prominent being a thin long one that stretches from the right side of his mouth up to his right ear. Those of us who have been here longer know he got that scar the day he tried to fight Banda. No one who knows Banda fights Banda. You are looking to get killed if you do. I can't remember what led to the quarrel. I arrived to hear Banda screaming, 'Ka fita harka na fa!' Stay out of my business! Banda never shouts so I knew this was not a small matter. Gobedanisa must have smoked a lot of the wee-wee Banda gave him. He uttered the unforgivable insult: 'Gindin maman ka!' Your mother's cunt! Banda was bigger than him and had a talisman and three amulets on his right arm for knives and arrows. Nothing made out of metal could pierce him.

As Gobedanisa insulted Banda's mother, Banda dropped from the guava tree branch he was sitting on and punched him right in the mouth. He was wearing his rusty ring with the sharp edges. Gobedanisa's mouth started bleeding. He picked up a wooden plank and rammed it into Banda's back. Banda looked back and walked off, to the tree. But Gobedanisa was looking for glory. Whoever could break Banda would be feared by the rest of us. We would follow that one. He picked a second plank and aimed for Banda's head but Banda turned quickly and blocked the blow with his right arm. The plank broke in two. Gobedanisa lunged with his bloodied hands and hit Banda on the jaw. Banda didn't flinch. No one separates fights in Bayan Layi except if someone is about to be killed or if the fight is really unfair. Sometimes, even then, we just let it go on because no one dies unless it is Allah's will. Banda grabbed Gobedanisa by the shirt, punched him twice in the face and twisted his right arm, which was reaching for a knife in his pocket. He pinned Gobedanisa to the ground and with his right fist made a long tear across his cheek.

No one holds a grudge in Bayan Layi. Gobedanisa still has his scar but he follows Banda and does what Banda says. Everything that happens is Allah's will, so why should anyone keep a grudge?

I like Banda because he is generous with his wee-wee. He doesn't like the way I tell him things that happen when he is away in Sabon Gari in the centre of town. He says I don't know how to tell a story, that I just talk without direction, like the harmattan wind that just blows and blows, scattering dust. Me, I just like to say it as I remember it. And sometimes you have to explain the story. Sometimes the explanation lies in many stories. How else can the story be sweet if you do not start it from its real, real beginning?

Banda gets a lot of money now that it is election season: to put up posters for the Small Party and tear off the ones for the Big Party or smash up someone's car in the city. He always shares his money with the boys and gives me more than he gives the rest. I am the smallest in the gang of big boys in Bayan Layi and Banda is the biggest. But he is my best friend.

Last month, or the month before Ramadan I think, this boy tried to steal in Bayan Layi. No one dares to come steal in Bayan Layi. Because it is a small community, it is easy to detect a stranger who is loitering. The boy tried to take some gallons of groundnut oil from Maman Ladidi's house. Her house is ba'a shiga: men aren't allowed to enter. She saw him and screamed. Then he ran and jumped over the fence. I like chasing thieves especially when I know they are not from Bayan Layi. I am the fastest runner here even though I broke my leg once when I fell from a motorcycle in Sabon Gari. Anyway, the groundnut oil thief, we caught him and gave him the beating of his life. I like using sharp objects when beating a thief. I like the way the blood spurts when you punch. So we sat this boy down and Banda asked what his name was. He said Idowu. I knew he was lying because he had the nose of an Igbo boy. I grabbed a long nail and pierced his head many times, demanding his real name.

'Idowu! I swear my name is Idowu,' he screamed as the nail tore into his flesh.

'Where is your unguwa?' Acishuru, the boy with one bad eye, asked, slapping him across the cheek. He knew how to slap, this boy with one bad eye.

'Near Sabon Gari,' the thief said.

'Where exactly?' I shouted. He kept quiet and I punched him in the neck with my nail.

'Sabon Layi.'

Then he just got up and ran, I tell you. Like a bird in the sky he just flew past us. We couldn't catch him this time. Banda asked us to leave him alone. He didn't reach Sabon Layi. Someone saw his body in a gutter that evening. See how Allah does things—we didn't even beat him too much. We have beaten people worse, wallahi, and they didn't die. But Allah chooses who lives and who dies. Not me. Not us.

The police came to our area with the vigilante group from Sabon Gari and we had to run away. Some hid in the mosque. Banda, Acishuru, Dauda and I swam across the river Kaduna, a part of which flows behind Bayan Layi, and wandered in the farms and bushes until it was late, too late to make it back across the river. Banda is not allowed to enter the river at night with his amulets. He says he will lose the power if the river water touches them at night and he cannot take them off because that too will kill their power.

Everyone is talking about the elections, how things will change. Even Maman Ladidi, who doesn't care about much apart from selling her groundnut oil, has the poster of the Small Party candidate on the walls of her house. She listens to her small radio for news about the elections. Everybody does. The women in the market wear wrappers carrying the candidate's face and the party logo, and many men are putting on white caftans and red caps just like him. I like the man. He is not a rich man but he gives plenty of alms and talks to people whenever he is in town. I like more the way he wears his red cap to the side almost like it's about to fall. I will get a cap like that if I get the money, maybe a white caftan too. But white is hard to keep clean—soap is expensive and the water in the river will make it brown even when you wash it clean. Malam Junaidu, my former Quranic teacher, wears white too and he says the Prophet, sallallahu alaihi wasallam, liked to wear white. But Malam Junaidu gives his clothes to the washman, who buys water from the boys who sell tap water. Some day, insha Allah, I will be able to buy tap water or go to the washman and have a box for all my white clothes. Things will be better if the Small Party wins. Insha Allah.

I like the rallies. The men from the Small Party trust Banda and they give him money to organise boys from Bayan Layi for them. Sometimes we get as much as one hundred fifty naira depending on who it is or which rally. We also get a lot to drink and eat.

I like walking around with Banda. The men respect him and even boys bigger than him are afraid of him. Banda became my friend two years ago, about the time I finished my Quranic training in Malam Junaidu's islamiyya. When I finished, Malam said I could go back to my village in Sokoto. Then Alfa, whose father lives near my father's house in Sokoto, had just arrived at the school and told me my father had died months earlier. I did not ask him what killed him because, Allah forgive me, I did not care much. It had been very long since I saw my father and he had not asked after me. Alfa said my mother still left the village every Friday to beg by the Juma'at mosque in Sokoto city and I had twin sisters whose names he didn't know. So, I told Malam Junaidu I was going back to Sokoto even though in my heart I didn't want to go. I thought he would give me the fare. It was three hundred naira from the park not too far away in Sabon Gari to get a space in the back of the trucks which carry wood to Sokoto. Instead he gave me seventy naira, reminding me that my father had not brought any millet that year or the year before to pay for my Quranic training. I had been there six years, and when I told him my father had died, he paused for a moment, then said 'Innalillahi wa inna ilaihi raji'un' and walked away. It is not that I didn't agree that it is Allah who gives life and who takes, it is the way he said it in that dry tone he used when teaching that made me sad. But I did not cry. I did not cry until that evening when I heard Alfa telling some boys I was a cikin shege. A bastard pregnancy. I don't know where he got that idea from. They were sitting by the well near the open mosque Malam Junaidu built. I kicked Alfa on the thigh and we started fighting. Normally I would have just beaten him up but two boys held me down so Alfa could keep slapping me. I was kicking and crying when Banda passed by. Everyone in Bayan Layi knew Banda. With one punch, Banda knocked Alfa down and flung one of the boys to the ground. I ran after Alfa and kept punching him in the stomach until my hands began to hurt. The other boys ran away. That day, I cried like I had never cried before. I followed Banda and he gave me the first wee-wee I ever smoked. It felt good. My legs became light and after a while I felt them disappear. I was floating, my eyes were heavy and I felt bigger and stronger than Banda and Gobedanisa and all the boys under the kuka tree. He said he liked the way I didn't cough when I smoked it. That was how we became friends. He gave me one of his flat cartons and took me to where they slept. They slept on cartons under the kuka tree and when it rained they moved to the cement floor in front of Alhaji Mohammed's rice store, which had an extended zinc roof. I cannot say when I decided to join the boys under the kuka tree. At first I still wanted to go back home, but as each day passed, I lost the desire to do so.

Banda was never an almajiri like me. He was born in Sabon Gari like most of the other boys but didn't attend Quranic school. Malam Junaidu had warned us about the kuka tree boys, who come to the mosque only during Ramadan or Eid days—'yan daba, thugs, who do nothing but cause trouble in Bayan Layi.' We despised them because they did not know the Quran and Sunna like us and did not fast or pray five times a day. 'A person who doesn't pray five times a day is not a Muslim,' Malam Junaidu would say. Now that I am also under the kuka tree, I know they are just like me and even though they don't pray five times a day, some of them are kind, good people—Allah knows what is in their hearts.

Banda is an old boy. I don't know how old, but he is the only one with a moustache among us. I hate it when people ask me my age because I don't know. I just tell them I have fasted nearly ten times. Some people understand when I say so, but others still ask annoying questions, like the woman during the census last year. But since the recent voter registration I have been saying I am nineteen, even though I have to fold the sleeves of the old caftan Banda gave me. The men in the Small Party asked us to say so and gave us all one hundred naira to register and even though the people registering us complained, they registered us anyway. My head was so big in the picture on the voter card, Banda and Acishuru kept laughing at me. I don't like it when Acishuru laughs at me because he has one bad eye and shouldn't be laughing at my head. He is so stingy he doesn't even like to share his wee-wee.

'We have a lot of work to do for the elections,' Banda says, coughing. Banda hasn't coughed like this before, spitting blood.

The Small Party has promised we may even get one thousand naira per head if they win the elections. They will build a shelter for us homeless boys and those who can't return home or don't have parents, where we can learn things like making chairs and sewing caftans and making caps.

Acishuru, Banda, Gobedanisa and I have been going with some boys from Sabon Gari to the Small Party office to talk about how to win the elections. No one likes the Big Party here. It is because of them we are poor. Their boys don't dare come here because people will drive them out.

Banda is coughing and spitting out even more blood. I worry. Maybe after the elections, when the Small Party becomes the Big Party, they can pay for him to go to the big hospital in the capital with plenty of flowers and trees. Or, if Allah wills it, he will get better without even needing the hospital.

It is about one hour after the last evening prayer and the Small Party man's brother has just driven into Bayan Layi in a white pickup truck with the party flag in front. He shouts Banda's name. Banda drops from the guava tree and I follow him.

'Which one of you is Banda?' a man asks from behind the truck. I can't see his face.

'I am,' Banda replies.

'And this one, who is he?'

'He's my friend; we sleep in the same place.'

'My name is Dantala,' I add.

'Well, we want just Banda.'

I am angry but I don't say a word.

'I am coming,' Banda says to me, adjusting the amulets on his right arm. It is his way of telling me he will be OK. He hops onto the back of the truck and they drive off.

Banda appears just as the muezzin sings the first call to prayer. It is election day. I didn't sleep because I was anxious and I knew they would give him a lot of money for the boys.

'What did they tell you?' I ask.

'Nothing.'

'What do you mean, nothing?' I am getting irritated. 'So they kept you all night for nothing?'

Banda doesn't say anything. He brings out two long wraps of wee-wee and gives one to me. We call it jumbo, the big one. He also hands me two crisp one hundred naira notes. I have not seen crisp notes like these in a long time.

'After prayers we will gather all the boys behind the mosque and give them one hundred fifty each. Then we wait. The party men will tell us what to do. Those who have their voters' cards will get an extra two hundred and I will collect all the cards and take them to their office.'

I am not sure why they have told Banda to collect the cards because I imagine they want us to help vote the Big Party out. But I want the extra two hundred. I am excited about the elections and the way everybody in Bayan Layi and even Sabon Gari likes the Small Party. They will surely win. Insha Allah!

Banda and I head for the polling centre between Bayan Layi and Sabon Gari even though we will not be voting. The day is moving slowly and the sun is hot very early. I hope the electoral officers come quickly so it can begin. Plenty of women are coming out to vote and the Small Party people are everywhere. They are handing out water and zobo and giving the women salt and dry fish in little cellophane bags. Everyone is cheerful, chatting in small groups. The Big Party agent arrives in a plain bus and takes off his party tag as soon as he gets there. I think he is afraid he will be attacked. He doesn't complain about the things the Small Party people are doing; he can't, because not even the two policemen can save him if he does. He knows, because he used to live in Bayan Layi too before he started working for the Big Party and moved to get a room in Sabon Gari. Banda says he hardly stays there and he spends most of his time in the capital where all the money is.

The voting is about to end and my wee-wee is wearing off, but I still have some left from the jumbo Banda gave me in the morning. I am hungry and tired of drinking the zobo that has been going around. I can't see Banda anywhere. I turn the corner of the street and find him bent over, coughing, holding his chest. He is still spitting a lot of blood. I ask him if he is OK. He says nothing, just sits on the floor, panting. I get him one sachet of water. He rinses his mouth and drinks some of it.

'We will win these elections,' Banda says.

'Of course, who can stop us?' We are talking like real politicians now, like party men.

'Will they really build us that shelter?' I ask.

'I don't like to think of that; all I want is that they pay every time they ask us to work for them. After the election, where will you see them?'

I am thinking Banda is very wise and I should stop expecting anything from the Small Party men. I light what is left of the jumbo and ask Banda if he wants some.

We hear screaming and chanting. The counting is over and as we expected, the Small Party has won here. I don't think the Big Party has more than twenty votes in this place. We get up and join the crowd, chanting, dancing and beating empty gallons with sticks.

I am exhausted. I slow down. I am still high and all these thoughts are suddenly going through my head—my mother who is far away, how I have hardly prayed since I left my Quranic teacher and how we only go to the Juma'at mosque in Sabon Gari on Fridays because there are people giving alms and lots of free food. But Allah judges the intentions of the heart. We are not terrible people. When we fight, it is because we have to. When we break into small shops in Sabon Gari, it is because we are hungry, and when someone dies, well, that is Allah's will.

Banda disappears again. He comes back early in the morning and says we have to be out again today after the morning prayers.

'We have been cheated in the elections,' Banda says, coughing and frantic.

'They have switched the numbers. We have to go out.'

I am still sleepy even though there is a lot of noise around. There are unfamiliar boys standing behind the mosque, shouting. I just want to sleep. My stomach is rumbling and my head hurts. This is the moment we have all been paid for. I had hoped all this would end last night. Unlike the other boys, I am not used to this breaking and burning business. Under the kuka tree, nothing is complete without some fire and broken glass.

'These Southerners can't cheat us, after all we are in the majority.'

I don't know the boy who is shouting, but he is holding a long knife. There are no Southerners here, I think, why is he holding out his knife? We all have knives here. I suck my teeth. The crowd is agitated. Banda looks like he can barely stand and is walking towards a parked pickup truck—the same pickup truck the Small Party people came in the other day. I see him bent down talking to someone inside the truck. Banda is just nodding and I wonder what he is being told. He walks back with his hands in the pockets of his old brown jallabiya. He comes into the crowd and whispers to the boy waving his knife in the air. The boy starts calling the crowd to order.

'We are going to teach them a lesson,' he says. 'We must scatter everything belonging to the Big Party in Bayan Layi.'

I must ask Banda who this boy is.

'Burn their office!' Gobedanisa shouts.

The crowd screams. I have always wanted to enter that office. I hear they keep money there. I scream with the crowd.

Banda tells us there are machetes, daggers and small gallons of fuel in the back of the truck. We will get two hundred naira each for taking back the votes that were stolen. Two hundred sounds nice. I can buy bread and fried fish. I haven't had fish in a while.

We file past the truck to get our two hundred naira notes and fuel and matches and machetes. The man handing out the notes doesn't talk. He just looks sternly into our eyes and hands out the notes. He gives a hundred to the smaller boys. I push out my chest as I approach the man, raising my chin so I don't look so small. I want the two hundred. The man looks at me and pauses, assessing me to see if I should get one or two hundred.

'We are together,' Banda says from behind me to the man. The man is not convinced and hands me a one hundred naira note. I take it—I never refuse money—and collect a machete from behind the truck. Banda whispers something to the man and then collects a note. He stretches it out to me—it is another one hundred naira note. I am glad and suddenly the sleep has cleared from my eyes. This is why I like Banda: he fights for me. He is a good person. He gives me something rolled up and wrapped in black polythene and asks me to hold it for him. It is money. I am not sure how much.

The first thing we do is set ablaze the huge poster of the Big Party candidate in front of the market. I like how the fire eats up his face. I wish it was his face in real life. The Big Party office is on my mind—I can't wait to search the offices and drawers and take whatever I can get from there before we set it ablaze.

I am the first to get to the Big Party office. The others are trailing closely behind me. They are excited, delirious, partly because we have been paid and partly because they hate the Big Party and are angry about the news we have heard.

We push the gate until we bring it down, together with the pillars to which it is attached. Tsohon Soja is the old man guarding the place. He tries to struggle with some of the boys, grabs one of them by the neck and blows his whistle. Another boy snatches the whistle from his mouth.

'You are an old man, Tsohon Soja, we don't want to harm you. Just stand back and let us burn this place down,' I tell him.

This security man is stubborn. He is a retired soldier and thinks he can scare us away. He reaches for his long stick and hits one of the boys on the shoulder. Gobedanisa charges forward with his machete, striking him on the chest and on the neck. None of the boys wanted to be the first to hit the old man because they all know him. Now that he is down they strike at his body. Me, I think it's bad luck to be killing such an old man. But he brought it upon himself. I know Gobedanisa will boast about this.

I run into the building; a boy in front of me has already opened the front door. I hope there is some money in the office—there must be—why else would the security man be trying to fight a whole crowd? We all enter the place, destroying furniture, tearing papers and posters, searching drawers. We go from room to room. All I can get is a transistor radio in one of the drawers. Acishuru gets a really new prayer mat and a cap. I am disappointed.

Banda is holding a half-gallon keg of petrol and so is the other boy who was wielding the knife behind the mosque.

'Get out, we are burning the place!' Banda orders.

I put the transistor radio in my other pocket—not the one with Banda's money—and it falls through to the ground. There is a big hole in my pocket. The radio has a little rope. I hang it around my neck and pick up my machete. I am also holding the matches, so I wait for them to finish pouring petrol while the other boys run out to the next building or billboard belonging to the Big Party.

'Pour more, pour more,' Banda tells the boy.

'No, this is enough; we need it for other places. It is petrol not kerosene.'

Banda concedes. I wait for them to come out. I strike a match and throw. The boy was right. I love the way the fire leaps out of the window and reaches for the ceiling. I remember when I was very small, my father almost beat me to death because I burnt a whole bag of millet stalks. That was before the rain stopped falling in our village and my father sent me and my three brothers far away for Quranic training. I don't know where they are now, my brothers. Maybe they have gone back home. Maybe they have decided to stay like me.

A fat man runs out of the burning building, towards me, covered in soot, coughing and stumbling over things. He can't see well. A Big Party man.

'Traitor!' one boy shouts.

The man is running with his hands in the air like a woman, like a disgusting 'dan daudu. I hate that he is fat. I hate his party, how they make us poor. I hate that he was hiding like a rat, fat as he is. I strike behind his neck as he stumbles by me. He crashes to the ground. He groans. I strike again.

The machete is sharp. Sharper than I expected. And light. I wonder where they got them from. Malam Junaidu's machetes were so heavy, I hated it when we had to clear weeds in front of the mosque or his house or his maize farm.

The man isn't shaking much. Banda picks up the gallon and pours some fuel on the body. He looks at me to strike a match. I stare at the body. Banda seizes the matchbox from me. The man squirms only a little as the fire begins to eat his clothes and flesh. He is dead already.

I am not thinking as we move on, burning, screaming, cutting, tearing. I don't like the feeling in my body when this machete cuts flesh, so I stick to the fire and take back the matchbox from Banda. At first we make a distinction between shops belonging to Big Party people and those belonging to Small Party people, but as we become thirsty and hungry, we just break into any shop we see.

As the crowd moves beyond Bayan Layi, they are stopped by the sound of gunfire ahead. I am still far behind taking a piss and I see the crowd running back. Two police vans are heading this way and they are firing into the air. As they get closer the policemen get out and start firing into the crowd. As I see the first person go down, I turn and run. I look back for Banda. He is not running. He is bent over, coughing, holding his chest. I stop.

'Banda, get up!' I scream, crouching behind a low fence.

Everyone is running past him and the police keep shooting. He tries, runs feebly and stops again. They are getting closer—Banda has to get up now. I want to run; I want to hope his amulets will work. But I linger a bit. He gets up again and starts to run. Then he falls flat on his face like someone hit him from behind. He is not moving. I run. I cut through the open mosque avoiding the narrow, straight road. I run through Malam Junaidu's maize farm. There are boys hiding there. I do not stop. I run past the kuka tree. I will not stop even when I can no longer hear the guns. Until I get to the river and across the farms, far, far away from Bayan Layi.

Sokoto

Apart from a big renovated expressway leading into the capital, Sokoto hasn't changed much. Even though the rains have not started yet, the rice farms of Fadama farmers stretch out like a shiny green cloth. Sometimes we pass millet or tobacco fields. Sometimes it is just bare, dry earth, broken up like my dreams every time I fall asleep on the way. Every time we pass a camel, I feel like reaching out and touching its long, lean neck. Camels look sleepy to me, like they are being forced to do everything when they are tired.

I thought a lot on my way to this dusty city as I sat with two other boys behind the lorry that carried wooden planks of various sizes. Once I thought a bad thought, astaghfirullah. I am ashamed to admit it, but I thought that if Allah was going to take someone, it should not have been Banda. I thought maybe Gobedanisa, or even Alfa should have been the one shot in Bayan Layi. This thought stayed with me for a long time until suddenly a fear gripped me in my chest for questioning Allah and why Banda was destined to die. So I kept saying astaghfirullah, Allah forgive me, until I noticed the other boys were looking at me like I had gone mad: what I was thinking had left my heart and started coming out of my mouth, goose bumps were all over my arms and I was shaking like I had a fever. My head was heavy. My back was aching from sitting for many hours on wood on the bumpy road.

Then suddenly the lorry began veering from left to right until one of its back tyres behind came off and we started going down a slope and into the bush. We were all screaming because the planks were falling out of the lorry. I held onto one big plank as the lorry tumbled down. Next thing I knew, the plank I held slid out of my hands and before I could let go of it, I was in the grass on cow dung, with bruised elbows and knees. I got up feeling dizzy and saw that the lorry had been stopped by a tree farther down the slope. I walked over the many planks strewn all over the place to where the lorry was, on its side. The driver and one of the two men sitting in front, who both had blood all over their bodies, were trying to pull the third man from the passenger seat. His head had gone through the glass and he wasn't moving. They dragged him out and shouted his name.

'Bilyaminu!'

Now that I think of it, I wish I didn't hear his name, because when I close my eyes, I hear his name and see his swollen head and all the blood. It makes me want to scream.

I mentioned the boys at the back of the truck to the men, who were using leaves to fan Bilyaminu. The driver got up and ran to the back. I ran with him. We didn't see the boys. Then we looked and saw blood under one of the planks still inside the lorry. I helped him lift the planks one by one. The driver screamed when he saw the legs of one of the boys. There was still a lot of wood piled up on their bodies. The second man, whose arm was broken, ran to the road to stop other cars to help us. Other lorries and buses stopped. The people from the village near the road also came out to help. When we had finally managed to remove all the planks I couldn't recognise either of them. I cried, without tears in my eyes, until my chest hurt. They were both almajirai like I was, returning home from their Quranic school to help their parents with harvesting. I don't know where they came from but they were not from Bayan Layi. Everyone agreed that it was best to bury the boys and that the driver, who said he knew their homes, would take the news to their parents. The villagers dug three graves not very far from the road and called their imam to say a prayer for the two boys and Bilyaminu.

The driver suggested that I join one of the other Sokoto-bound lorries which had stopped. As I washed up at a well in the village I realised I still had Banda's polythene wrap of money, but I couldn't find the other notes I had in my front pocket. I was glad that I didn't ask the two boys their names. It makes it easier to forget.

I am dizzy as I walk through the motor park in Sokoto. My lips are cracked and bleeding. I can't decide what to do or if I want to go home yet to look for my mother. There are mango trees near the shops inside the park and I go under one to lie down. It is cool here but there are many ants—the red ones that can make you scream and jump when they bite. I crush a few around me before Bayan Layi invades my thoughts. I bring out the wrapped money and count it, looking around to make sure no one is watching. I count in Arabic. This is one thing Malam Junaidu taught us well. Sometimes, during our lessons, he spoke only in Arabic and if we did not understand he would lash us with a whip made from old motorcycle tyres. I didn't get beaten much for Arabic, because I learned very fast. I never forget a thing once I have memorised it.

I can't believe how much is in this wrap. Eight thousand three hundred naira. The most money I have ever had is three hundred fifty naira, which Banda gave me from one of the rallies and even then I considered myself rich. I divide the money into three parts. Three hundred naira I put in my front pocket, five hundred naira I put in my right trousers pocket and seven thousand five hundred I wrap in the polythene and put in my left trousers pocket. My head is pounding and my bruises are getting sore. My whole body is trembling like when I was thinking bad thoughts towards Allah in the lorry. My stomach is twisting and biting. I think that I did not die in the lorry because I quickly realised my sin and said astagh-firullah many times. I wonder about those two boys, whose bodies were not even whole bodies when we found them beneath those wooden planks. But Allah knows why—it is all destined by Him.

I see an open chemist. I walk into the store and meet many other people there. Everyone calls the store owner Doc-tor but one man calls him Chuks. He is short and his eyeballs look like they are about to fall out. I wonder if the skin over his eyes can cover them completely when he sleeps or if there will still be some eye left. His fingers are short and fat and he scratches his large belly with his hand as he talks. He is fair-skinned, not fair like a city Fulani, but like the muddy puddles in Bayan Layi after it rains. I can't stop looking at his huge nose, which seems to be divided into three parts. He must be breathing in a lot of air.

'Ehen, what do you want?' he says, breathing hard.

'I am not well,' I say.

'You are not well? What is doing you?' His Hausa is funny and the more I stare at it, his nose is like the nose of the thief who lied saying his name was Idowu.

'My head hurts and I have thrown up and my stomach is turning and my body is trembling,' I tell him. I remember the accident and I add, 'and I fell from a lorry and hurt my elbows and knees.'

'Do you have money?'

He looks at me from head to toe when he asks this. I am getting dizzier and irritated at his questions. I want to tell him that he should not mind that my clothes are dirty and my slippers are different colours and worn out—that I probably have more money in my pocket than he does in the little wooden box where he takes change from, that I can buy anything in his store. But I want to be treated so I just tell him, 'Yes, I have money.'

'Your headache and trembling, is it before or after you fell from the car?'

'It was a lorry, not a car.'

'Look here, is it me or you who is doing the treatment? What concerns me whether it is lorry or airplane or bicycle? Do you want me to treat you or not?'

'Sorry.'

'Before or after!'

'Before.'

He hisses and goes into a wooden cubicle inside the shop. He comes out with a bag and asks me to come inside. I want to tell him that it really started when I thought bad thoughts towards Allah, but I am sure he is not a Muslim. He asks me to roll up my sleeves and trousers and uses scissors to dip cotton wool in a bottle. As the cotton wool begins to foam on my skin it stings me and I flinch and knock the scissors out of his hand. He screams at me saying that if I do not sit still he will send me away and I will still pay for the cotton wool he has wasted. I sit still, close my eyes and grit my teeth as he takes out new cotton wool and applies all the other things which hurt even more. Then he brings out a syringe and needle and draws out some medicine from three different little bottles until the syringe is almost full.

'Have you eaten?' he asks.

'No.'

'Are you a fool? Do you want to collapse when I give you this injection? Go and eat something outside now if you have money. Do you have another money?'

'Yes.'

I walk out and buy a sachet of kunu from one of the girls in the park and then some bread from the store next to the chemist. There are buses going to my village, Dogon Icce; I hear the conductors shout for passengers. I think of my mother, who I left so long ago. I don't know what I will do if I go back. My mind drifts from there to the kuka tree in Bayan Layi and I wonder if there are still policemen in the area. Chuks interrupts my thoughts and tells me to hurry up. I stuff the remaining bread in my mouth and go in.

I can feel the kunu rising in my stomach right after the injection and I run out to throw up. Everything around me is double and I feel a hand grabbing me before everything begins to fade.

I wake up and find that I have been sleeping on a bench inside the chemist. It is dark outside and I am drenched in sweat.

'How are you feeling now?' Chuks asks.

'Better, but my head hurts still.'

'Here, take this and make sure you eat something before you sleep. Your money is three hundred seventy naira.'

He gives me white tablets and tells me the entire treatment will finish in three days. Two more injections, he says.

Chuks reminds me of the fat man from the Big Party office. I think this as I pay him and then walk to the mosque in the motor park. There are taps there and I swallow the two large white tablets.

This mosque is nice. It smells newly painted. Outside the mosque there is smooth concrete pavement where the taps are. There are three doors, one in front for the imam, where he stands to sing the call to prayer, and two doors on either side. Inside at the back, there is a room with a wooden door which is locked. There are four ceiling fans and one big standing fan in the front right corner. The red wall-to-wall rug is bright and neat. I lie down in the mosque and begin to doze off until I feel a man tap me lightly.

'Won't you get up and say your prayers?' he says and walks away.

It is a command, not a question. His voice is deep and his beard is grey and black in a pattern so neat as if he coloured it himself. It is he who sings the call to isha prayer. His call makes one want to stop and listen to the words, and want to pray. It is deep and loud but smooth and gentle on the ears:

Allahu Akbar
Allahu Akbar
Allahu Akbar
Allahu Akbar . . .

I do my ablution outside by the taps and rush in, attaching myself to the end of the long row that has quickly formed. Shoulder to shoulder. Toe to toe. I have not prayed like this since the last Eid. It feels nice. 'Praying in congregation makes us equal before Allah,' Malam Junaidu liked to say, 'shoulder to shoulder.' Even though of course he did not treat us like we were equal to him. My knees hurt when I kneel to pray but I don't mind. I am praying next to a short person. I think he is a boy like me until I turn and see he has a long, thick beard.

The prayer is over and I am thinking of what to eat when this man who prayed by my side stretches his hand to me and says, 'Salamu alaikum.'

'Wa alaikum wassalam,' I reply.

His voice is bigger than he is and sounds as if it is coming from somewhere out of his body. I wonder if the beard is heavy for his face. He asks me if I have eaten and tells me that there is free food outside the mosque. I walk out to where the food is being shared and I see some men offloading sacks from behind a black jeep. The food is in small, disposable paper packs. Joining the rush to reach for food, I knock down a little boy. The man who dropped the sacks is shouting, asking us to wait, to calm down because there is enough to go round. No one is listening to him; no one wants to take a chance. Some people are taking as many as three packs. Others spill the contents of their packs as they try to run off with more than they can carry. I am able to get two packs before people empty the sacks.

The man was wrong. There is not enough to go round and many are left without. I walk back to the mosque with what I have got. Both packs have jollof rice in them but only one of them has a small piece of boiled meat. I see the little boy I knocked down, still on the ground crying. He didn't get any food. The bearded man who told me there was food is outside the mosque entrance, his short arms on his waist, looking at me and at the boy on the ground. His eyes are saying many things to me, the way my mother's, Umma's, eyes said many things when I did something wrong. Those eyes of hers were more painful than the knocks from my father's hard knuckles. I am ashamed and look to the ground avoiding the crying boy and the short man's gaze of judgment. I can still feel his eyes as I reluctantly squat and tap the boy, whose head is buried in his lap. He looks up. I give him the pack without meat. He wipes his eyes with the back of his left hand and receives the pack with his right. My eyes follow him as he gets up and walks away from the mosque into the darkness where there are broken-down buses and cars. He doesn't even say thank you.

The man is still standing there as I make my way towards the mosque, still looking at me, half-smiling now. His eyes are better, they commend me. I open the pack and eat the rice quickly before I will have to share it too. I chew hard upon a stone and it sends a shock through my body before I spit it out. There is hardly any salt in the rice and the meat is tough. It is easier to just swallow it.

The short man talks to me as I drink water at the tap.

'Allah will reward you for sharing your food, as Allah will reward and grant the wishes of Alhaji Usman, who sent the food,' he says and walks away.

My head is pounding and I feel like throwing up. I close the tap and walk into the mosque to lie down. There aren't many mosquitoes here even though the mosque has two open doors.

I lie on my back in the centre of the mosque, counting the number of squares on the ceiling. There are many people sitting in the mosque and they are all talking about the elections and the fighting in many places including Sabon Gari and Bayan Layi. People are outraged at the Big Party and the fact that the results of the elections have been changed. One man behind me says that it is our own people who have sold us out. He says this in response to another man with a tiny voice who said that the Southerners were attempting to take power away from our people, whose turn it is to rule. The man with the tiny voice doesn't talk again. The voice behind me continues.

'Our Emirs and big men are greedy and are not interested in us or our religion. They only claim to be Muslim and Northern but side with those oppressing us. For them an infidel party that accepts all sorts of kufr is more important than standing with Muslims and with Allah.'

I turn to look at who is speaking because when he speaks, everyone listens and nods. It is the small bearded man with the big voice.

I feel my pockets and realise I no longer have the polythene wrap of money. My other pocket still has the change left after I had paid Chuks the doctor and bought kunu and bread. My head is going round in circles and my heart is beating faster. I get up and look round the mosque, scanning the floor. I check by the tap, look in the gutter. Nothing. The scramble for food! I run out to check where we knocked each other over for rice. I run towards every black thing on the floor that looks like the polythene. Nothing. Only grains of jollof rice and empty paper packs. Tracing my steps back the way I came, I walk slowly, thankful for the bright fluorescent light outside the mosque. Then I see something familiar. I dive for it. My heart sinks as I realise it is really my polythene bag. Empty! I can't breathe and my head is pounding hard. The polythene wrap slips from my hand as I walk back slowly to the mosque. I am holding myself back from crying. A man asks me if I have lost something.

'Is it not you I am talking to?' he raises his voice.

I still do not answer. The man mutters something about 'children these days' and walks off. Who can I tell that some-one just took my seven thousand five hundred naira, which really belonged to a dead friend of mine who was shot by the police? How do I even start that story?

I enter the mosque and people are still discussing the elections. My eyes are tired from looking for my money and my head hurts. Perhaps if I wasn't so tired or sick or angry from having lost all my money I might have told them about Bayan Layi and the burnt Big Party office and the fat man that Banda set ablaze or Tsohon Soja, who Gobedanisa killed with his machete. I would not say that I was there, that I held a machete too or that I was the one who hit the Big Party man. I would say only that someone told me.

I lie down and block out all the voices. Flashes of blood and mangled bodies and fire are going through my head. Allah forgive me, but some wee-wee would be good right now so that I could forget these horrible images. If Banda were here he would have given me some; we would have sat down under the kuka tree and talked about things that didn't matter, until we fell asleep.

I wake up to a bitter taste in my mouth and the muezzin's call to prayer in my ear. My bones hurt so bad—my back, my knees, my neck, my arms—it feels like someone has beaten me with iron rods. I am trying to remember the dream I had. All I have are images that come and go. I saw Umma sitting on her little stool, with her back against the wall, beneath an old picture of Sheikh Inyass. She had dark circles around her eyes from my father always punching her in the face. She said many things to me which I can't remember. Her face was not happy. I saw Banda with a hole in his chest and blood around his mouth. It's the part about Umma I want to remember, especially what she told me. Maybe she has become old, I think, as I drag myself to the tap to perform ablution.

The small man with the big voice is at the tap, his eyes puffy from sleep. He is not talking and smiling like he was yesterday. He washes quickly and goes in to stand in front of the mosque behind the muezzin with the nicely patterned grey and black beard. Just before I go down on my knees, which still hurt a bit, I feel my pockets to make sure I still have my change left. A cold, light breeze blows from the door on my right just after I say, 'Allahu Akbar.' It feels like Allah hears my whisper, and answers. I can feel His greatness this morning and I am feeling sorry, for the first time, for all I have done. For smoking wee-wee. For breaking into shops with the kuka tree boys. For striking that man with a machete. For questioning Allah on my way back to Sokoto.

I sit down after the prayer to listen to the man with the grey and black beard preach. The tafsir is well attended and everyone listens as he talks of our duty as Muslims.

'This country is a slave to Jews and their usury,' he says. I am hearing of a World Bank and IMF for the first time. I understand the concept of a huge bank that gives loans to countries around the world but I don't understand what the IMF has to do with anything. Or what it is. Everyone else seems to know, because no one has asked and I am sure I will look stupid if I do. I just conclude it is a bad Jewish thing that helps the World Bank, who gives us money we don't need to enslave us.

'This is why the West pushes our leaders to make laws that force us to go to Western schools at an early age, so that they can teach our children that this system of the Jews is the best and by the time they learn otherwise it is too late.'

He says all this without shouting or speaking very fast like Malam Junaidu. He mentions the elections and there is slight murmuring in the audience after which follows complete silence. His voice is gentle but his words are piercing, giving me goose bumps.

'Allah will judge those who sell their brothers for money,' he says slowly, so that every word goes under your skin. The short man with the big voice walks in and whispers something into the ears of the Imam. Then the Imam says to us that Alhaji Usman has sent breakfast and those who want to eat can go outside. This Alhaji Usman must be very rich, I think.

I ask the man sitting next to me on the floor what the Imam's name is. Sheikh Jamal is the name of this man whose words have arrested my feet and gone under my skin. His deputy—the short man with the big voice—is Malam Abdul-Nur Mohammed.

'Abdul-Nur is not a Hausa man,' he confides to me.

'Really?'

'He is a Yoruba from Ilorin. In fact his name was Alex before he converted, learned Arabic and memorised the whole Quran in just one year. There is not a hadith of the Prophet that he doesn't know.'

I want to ask this man who seems to know everything about this Malam Abdul-Nur how he came about this information but I don't want to upset him. I listen to Sheikh Jamal some more before I go out to get the free breakfast. A huge luxury bus is setting out from the motor park and there are little curtains drawn over its windows. Someday I will ride in one of those, wherever they go to, I tell myself.

The food is all finished when I arrive. Two girls hawking rice cakes in small transparent plastic buckets watch in irritation as people disperse from the jeep that has brought sacks of food.

'Me, since they started bringing this sadaka, I have hardly sold much,' the bigger one says to the smaller one.

'Me neither,' the smaller one replies.

'I think tomorrow we should head somewhere else or into town.'

'Or where the motorcyclists wash their motorcycles.'

I feel someone touch my shoulder. It is Malam Abdul-Nur holding a plastic plate and bowl. He is smiling again.

'Did you get the food?' he asks.

'No,' I say, avoiding his eyes.

'Rinse the plates and bring them into the mosque when you finish,' he says, giving me the plate of kosai and bowl of hot koko.

He has taken many steps before my mouth can say 'thank you.' I will thank him when I return the plates. These are good people and if I didn't have to go home to my mother, I would stay here. My stomach rumbles as the hot koko rolls down my throat into my belly.

Umma! This koko tastes just like hers—the one she used to sell in front of our house and by the market in the village when the rains were regular and my father's rented farm gave many bags of millet and maize. I can't wait to see her again. She will ask me how it was in Bayan Layi and whether my teacher treated me well. I will tell her that everything was good so that she will smile and not worry and get the pain in her chest that my grandmother used to say was from too much thinking. It confused me then how something in the head could cause pain in the chest and my grandmother would say that while men worry with the head, women worry with the heart. When I would ask again, she would say I was too young to understand. Today I think my dead grandmother is wrong. It is not only women who get that pain in the chest. I feel it now—when I think of Umma and Banda—in my stomach, in my chest, in my head, everywhere.

I rinse the plates by the mosque taps and take them in to Malam Abdul-Nur. He is sitting with Sheikh Jamal. They look up at me.

'Yes, he's the one I was telling you about,' Malam tells Sheikh Jamal.

I give him the plates and say I am grateful.

'Sit,' he says.

I sit slowly trying not to bend my knees. Sheikh Jamal looks into my eyes searching—for what, I do not know. I look at him at first but can't stand the weight of his eyes. Suddenly I am aware of all the sounds in the room: the whirring of the fans, someone washing at the tap outside, the revving of cars about to set off on long journeys, the bus conductors outside screaming to potential passengers, someone laughing loudly in front of the mosque. Perhaps he can hear the beating of my heart, because I can, in spite of the many sounds.

'By what name are you called?' Sheikh Jamal's very formal tone breaks through all the sounds and blocks them out.

'Dantala. But my father named me Ahmad.'

During the very long silence all I can hear is his heavy breathing and the crunching of the fresh lobe of white kola nut which Malam Abdul-Nur has just popped into his mouth. There is something about the Sheikh which makes my heart beat faster. Faster in a good way, not faster like when I broke Umma's large mirror and heard her coming into the room. I can't tell what it is.

He pulls at the tip of his beard freeing entangled strands of hair. I want a beard like this. Maybe not with the grey hairs, but I like the way it covers most of his face and neck.

'You have a good name, the name of our Prophet, sallallahu alaihi wasallam.' He dims his eyes when he says, 'Peace be upon him.'

I nod.

Then Malam Abdul-Nur speaks, holding up his right palm like a slate, turning between me and Sheikh. 'But

Dantala . . . Dantala is not a name. To say someone was born on a Tuesday, is that a name? A name should have meaning. Like Ahmad, the name of the Prophet, sallallahu alaihi wasallam. You should stop using that Dantala.'

I keep nodding.

'Where is your home, the home of your father?' Sheikh continues.

'My father died, but he lived in Dogon Icce with my mother.'

'Allah is King! May Allah grant him rest. May Allah forgive his bad deeds and remember his good ones. May Allah reward him with aljanna.'

I say amen after every prayer.

'So what do you intend to do now?'

'I want to go to my mother in Dogon Icce. I fell sick when I came back from being an almajiri in Bayan Layi and was taking injections with the fair man on the other side of the motor park. Chuks.'

'Aha, the Igbo man. He is good. Are you feeling any better?'

'Yes. Very much.'

He pauses again and whispers something to Malam Abdul-Nur.

'What is the name of your teacher in Bayan Layi?' he asks.

'Malam Junaidu.'

He turns to Malam Abdul-Nur and asks, 'Is it our Junaidu?'

'I am sure it is,' Malam Abdul-Nur replies and then turns to me and asks: 'Isn't he very dark with a mark across his cheek?'

I nod. Sheikh Jamal takes out a phone from his front pocket. I am afraid. If he calls Malam Junaidu, then he will probably hear that I joined the kuka tree boys, who smoked wee-wee and didn't pray. He raises the phone to his ear and my heart beats faster, not in a good way.

He starts to talk and asks Malam Junaidu how he is, how his farm is going, and they go on and on about the rains and then about the violence and curfew in Bayan Layi. Then as if the question doesn't matter he asks if he ever had an almajiri named Ahmad who is also called Dantala. He describes me as quiet, not too dark, not too tall and very thin. As he listens to the reply, the ground on which I sit gets hotter and my stomach suddenly feels like my intestines are being tied together very tightly. I want to get up and run away. He nods and stares at me. After a while he says goodbye and lays down the phone.

'So when do you want to go to your mother?' he asks.

'When I finish the injections, I will go,' then I add, 'and when I have enough money.'

I wonder where I will go if Sheikh Jamal throws me out of this mosque. It costs six hundred fifty naira to get to my village from the motor park. I don't have that much. I wonder what he now knows: if he knows about Banda, about our burning of the Big Party office.

'Do you have anyone taking care of you?' he asks.

'No, no one,' I say, the words barely leaving my mouth.

'Do you like it here? Would you like to work with us?'

'Yes,' I say without thinking. My heart is back to beating faster in a good way.

'Finish your injections and go to your mother. Let her see you. The prophet teaches us to be kind to our parents, to help them. I am sure there are ways you can help her. Then ask her if you can come back. If she says yes, come back. But only if she says yes. We have two buses going to Dogon Icce: Malam Abdul-Nur will show you. You can join any of them when you are ready. He will give you some money to return also—if your mother lets you return. And if you decide to stay there, may Allah be with you.'

There is a pain deep in my nose because I am holding back my tears.

'Thank you,' I say snuffling.

Malam Abdul-Nur motions to me to leave. I get up. But I have to know what Malam Junaidu said.

'Please what did Malam Junaidu say?' I don't know where I get the boldness.

'He said you know your Arabic well.'

I walk away, relieved.

The day is just getting bright and Chuks is opening his store. As he struggles with his many padlocks I sit on the blackened bench outside. I think of all I would have said if the Sheikh had asked me about my mother. I try to imagine Umma now, fair, long face, deep dimples and dark circles round her eyes. She said her teeth were brown from the water they drank growing up. Her slender fingers and feet always have dark lalle tattoos on them. Sometimes they are reddish. Unlike her mother, Umma is slim and tall. She says she gets it from her father. He fell from a date palm tree when she was little. Umma is quiet and doesn't spend her time gossiping with any of the other women in Dogon Icce. She laughs softly when she does but mostly, her eyes are sad. I wonder what she thinks about when she sits by the zogale tree inside the house watching lizards run around or when she absently waves flies away from her body. Often when she complained that her chest hurt, my grandmother would tell her, 'You think too much. What is in this world?'

Chuks' shop is now open and I walk in. The thoughts of Umma make the pain not so bad when the needle enters my buttocks. It only matters now that I will be going home. To my mother. To her gentle smile and deep eyes.

Dogon Icce

I try to squeeze onto the makeshift seat in the middle of the Nissan bus. Because the seat usually gets hot, the bus conductor has some rags and plywood to sit on. He asks me if I am Malam's passenger and I say yes. He tells me to sit in front instead. The new motor park laws say that buses cannot have more than one passenger in the front seat. I have never travelled this comfortably before.

I have two big polythene bags, both from Malam Abdul-Nur and Sheikh: inside are three big mudus of millet flour, two big mudus of maize flour, a half mudu of sugar, a half mudu of salt, two used but still almost new caftans and three bars of soap. This is more food and possessions than I have ever had and I hold the polythene tightly refusing to let the conductor keep it in the back. Umma will be pleased. Her smile will be soft like she smiles when other women are jumping and screaming in celebration. She doesn't clap her hands or hold her nose to make that ringing noise that women like to make during weddings or naming ceremonies. The neighbours, unless they see me coming, won't know I am around from any noise in the house because her happiness will be in her face: I will see it in the wrinkles around her dark eyes, in the dimples in her cheeks. I don't know if she will hug me like she did before I left. I am much bigger now. Women only hug boys who are little.

Sheikh Jamal is standing at the motor park gate as we drive out.

'May Allah forgive Malam,' the driver greets him, slowing down.

'Salamu alaikum,' Sheikh Jamal replies stretching his hand to shake the driver's.

The driver receives the handshake with two hands, bowing slightly. Sheikh Jamal extends his hand to shake mine too and says, 'May Allah forbid a mishap on the road.'

'Amen,' I say and hear many people in the bus also whisper amen. Every prayer is important, especially that of an Imam. The road to Dogon Icce is horrible in several places and it is not strange to hear that there has been an accident.

On the way an old man starts talking about how his farm was destroyed by the rains and flooding. He has lost all his millet and maize, he says.

'You should be grateful to Allah you still have a roof over your head,' a younger man says. His house crumbled under the water and his entire family is without a home. One of the women at the back starts to cry as she tries to relate that her little son drowned when the waters came. Two other women console her.

I have no stories to share. I want to ask if anyone knows my mother, Umma, the fair Shua woman from Maiduguri who used to sell millet gruel by the market. If I had a picture of her, perhaps I would show them. The driver is silent. I ask him when the floods happened, and he says more than a month ago, surprised that I hadn't heard.

'Where have you been?' he asks.

'Bayan Layi,' I reply. Perhaps I should stop telling everyone where I am coming from.

'No wonder. The floods lasted many days: in fact we couldn't drive into Dogon Icce and all the surrounding villages until last week. Just two rains and the whole place is destroyed.'

People are dying of sickness, he complains. There is no water or hospital in Dogon Icce and many people, especially children, purge until they die. The water got contaminated after the flood and although the local government chairman promised to bring water tankers, they have not seen any yet.

Everyone is now talking at the same time and I can't follow anything. I think of Umma and her mud house and hope, insha Allah, that the house my father built when the millet farms gave many bags is still standing. I don't understand this flood business. The last I knew when I was in Dogon Icce was that there were no rains and millet was drying up in the farms except for the large farms owned by the brothers of one big man who had machines that pumped water from the rivers. Too little rain then, too much rain now.

There is a little old booklet on the dashboard. I ask the driver if I can have a look. He asks if I can read it, says it is a book in Hausa and Arabic. I smile. I want to tell him that when I was in Malam Junaidu's school, there were only three who knew how to read both Hausa and Arabic—I and two of Malam Junaidu's brothers, who sometimes taught us when he was away, that my mother speaks fluent Arabic though she cannot read, that I probably know it better than he does. I nod and pick up the book. The title is in Hausa: *100 Authentic Hadiths on How Muslims Should Conduct Themselves*. It is compiled by Mahmud Yunus. The pages on the left have the hadiths in Arabic while the pages on the right are in Hausa. I could memorise this book in an hour if I set my mind to it. It's been a long time since I did that; I have never memorised anything without a whip in front of me. As I start reading, it feels different. I look up to be sure there is no one holding a whip over my head. Reading is nice if someone is not forcing you to do it. The first hadith is familiar.

> Actions are but by intentions and every man shall have only that which he intended. Thus he whose migration was for Allah and His Messenger, his migration was for Allah and His Messenger, and he whose migration was to achieve some worldly benefit or to take some woman in marriage, his migration was for that for which he migrated.

The driver looks at me in amazement as I read under my breath but loud enough for him to hear. I am doing this deliberately and look at him, expecting him to ask where I learned to read or who my teacher is. He only shakes his head and smiles.

The driver taps me as we approach Dogon Icce junction. I wake up, wiping saliva that has rolled down the side of my mouth. It is crowded as usual with people trying to make their way into the villages around. The roads here are not like the roads in town. They are mostly narrow bush paths cleared by the villagers. The main road was cleared by a member of the House of Representatives who was building a big house in the village. He only comes briefly during the big Sallah and shares a lot of meat and grain.

'The motorcycles are not even agreeing to pass this road after the floods,' one woman with a baby on her back complains.

She and a few women are going to walk all the way to the village.

'You have to even take off your shoes most of the way,' another woman with a sack of grain says.

I walk behind the women as they complain about their losses. The woman with the baby has just returned from the hospital in Sokoto where her daughter has given birth but is still very ill.

'They say her waist was too small and she should not have gotten pregnant so early. I don't know what this world is becoming these days. When I had her, I was not up to her age. Did I even have breasts when I was married off? Yet I had all my children without any complaints. It must be the new fertilizer, I tell you. It's all poison, wallahi. When it was only cow dung, who heard about such things for Allah's sake? Imagine, they had to tear her open for the baby to come out! Even the baby is not doing well.'

The other women agree.

'May Allah lighten her burdens,' the woman with the grains on her head says.

'If only we had a hospital here, I wouldn't have to make this long journey back and forth to get her things, but no, if not buying cars, and sharing meat during elections and Sallah, there is nothing else they do. Tell me, for Allah's sake, what is a little meat when I have to travel to get to a hospital?'

If, insha Allah, I ever have the money, I will build a road to Dogon Icce and a hospital. And a nice mosque with a rug, like the new one at the motor park in Sokoto, but bigger. I would paint it completely white and build a concrete house for Umma by the side. I would give her all she needs and stop her from selling gruel or doing any work for that matter. Maybe then she would stop sitting and staring at lizards for long periods.

As we walk through a huge pool of thick muddy water the woman with the grain on her head slips and falls flat. The contents of her polythene bag spill into the mud. A few grains of wheat float while most sink to the bottom. It is too late to save any of it. She starts to cry as the other women take her by the hand to lift her up. There is nothing I can do to help her; both my hands are full and I am in the middle of the water. They are too busy trying to clean the woman up to hear me say sorry. I feel bad just walking past like this, without stopping. But Allah knows the intentions of my heart. That is all that counts.

I could have sworn my house stood here, where this mound of mud and thatch is. There is nothing I recognise. An old man chops off wood from a fallen tree ahead. The axe seems too heavy for him and he groans with every strike at the trunk of the tree. He stops when he notices me.

'What are you looking for?' he asks.

'My house. My mother's house,' I tell him.

'Who is your mother?'

'Umma.'

'Umma, mai koko?'

They still call her the one who sells gruel. When I say yes, he looks away and sighs. I am scared. I drop the bags I am holding.

'That is her house you are looking at. Her sister-in-law took her to Katako. Do you know where it is?'

'Yes,' I reply and pick up my bags. Katako is a bit far from here but there is a shortcut through Dogon Icce. As I walk away, he says something I do not hear. I do not stop. All I want is to see my mother.

The only houses standing are the few made of concrete blocks. Many trees have fallen, some uprooted from the ground. I hope, insha Allah, I find Umma well. Without walls or trees to climb, there are so many lizards on the ground looking like they have lost their way. My feet hurt from walking but I will not stop to rest. It is evening and I want to reach Katako before the sun goes down. There are flies everywhere and bloated carcasses of dogs and goats. The smell in the village makes my stomach rumble. Now I feel like I should have left for Dogon Icce as soon as I arrived in Sokoto. Only Allah knows why this happened, why my mother's house is now a huge pile of mud and thatch. I wonder if any of my brothers are back. If I had a phone like Sheikh Jamal or Malam Junaidu and I could get one for Umma and my brothers, I would have called them to know how they were and where they were. All I know is that when the rains first stopped falling and the millet dried up in the farm, my father sent them—Maccido, Hassan and Hussein—to become almajirai in an Islamic school in a place called Tashar Kanuri. A few months after, I was off to Bayan Layi because the malam in Tashar Kanuri didn't have space for more students. I wonder why Umma didn't send anyone to look for me when my father died or if my brothers knew. Allah knows. Allah knows what is best.

The day my brothers left for Tashar Kanuri, I was both sad and happy. Sad that suddenly I didn't have anyone to protect me from the bullies in the village but happy I had more space to sleep and maybe my portions of food would become bigger. The portions never got bigger. Maccido used to slap me hard for no reason, even though Umma used to quarrel with him about it. He never listened to her and was mean because he was the eldest and was bigger than all of us. Still, he beat up anyone who beat me or tried to bully me in the village. Sometimes I liked him. Sometimes I hated him. Hassan and Hussein, the twins, were quiet and fair like Umma. Many times I thought Umma loved them more than she loved the rest of us. Nobody beat or bullied them. Umma told us my father only beat them to make them change from being left-handed when they were very little. So they learned how to use their right hands but didn't stop using their left hands. I always wished I knew how to use both hands. Nobody believed Hassan and Hussein could do any wrong, so when they would go to play with Maccido and come back late, my father would beat only Maccido. My father wanted to send just Maccido and Hassan to Tashar Kanuri but everyone thought it was a bad idea to separate the twins, so he sent all three of them leaving me alone with Umma.

I stop and rub my palms together. They are red from carrying the two bags. I can see my aunt's mud house in the distance and my heart is beating fast. Tears are filling my eyes and my nose hurts. I can't remember the last time I was here but little has changed apart from the roof, which is no longer thatch but old rusted zinc. There is also now a reed curtain covering the door that leads into the zaure, the room at the entrance where male visitors are received.

'Salamu alaikum,' I shout at the entrance.

'Wa alaikum wassalam. Who is it?' The man who answers sounds angry.

The man walks into the zaure from the house and looks into my face. It is my aunt's husband, Shuaibu.

'Allah be praised!' he shouts.

I smile.

'Dantala! When did you get into town? But you have not been fair, wallahi. Are you the first to be sent away to be an almajiri? Your brothers have been coming, but you, no. What happened to you?'

I don't know which of his questions to answer first or why he is shouting at me.

'Anyway, stop standing there like a stranger, go in and let them give you water to wash up.'

I walk through, more scared than I have ever been, sad that Umma might think I have let her down.

'Khadija,' he shouts, 'come and relieve Dantala, he has some things with him.'

'Which Dantala?' Khadija screams and runs out of her room.

I cannot look into her eyes as she screams 'inna lillahi wa inna ilaihi raji'un' several times. She grabs me, hugs me and starts to cry. She drags me by the hand into her room.

'Come and let your mother see your face, maybe she will agree to say something. Since she lost her girls she has stopped talking or eating. We have to force her to eat.'

My eyes widen.

'Oh Allah! You never even met your sisters ko? Cute little things, wallahi.'

I am too confused to say anything.

'I am on my way out, I will be back soon,' Shuaibu says, standing outside the room.

'Toh, see you later,' Khadija says, wipes her tears and opens the window for light to come in. The sun has just started setting. The first thing I see is Umma's legs. She is lying with her face to the wall.

'Get up, Umma, see Dantala is here, he is back.' Khadija taps Umma lightly on the shoulder.

Umma rolls over, picks up her scarf and covers her head. Tears are rolling down my face.

'Umma,' I say, my voice trembling.

She looks up at me, smiles and without saying a word gets up and leaves the room. I can't believe my own Umma will not say a word to me.

We follow her out to the little courtyard where she is now sitting, staring up at the sky. Khadija is crying and telling me this is how she has been. That she lost my sisters in the flood—she doesn't know where the water took them—their bodies have not been found. I learn for the first time that my twin sisters were called Hassana and Husseina. That they were fair and beautiful and looked like my father. That they comforted Umma after she lost my father and she loved them more than anything in the world since her boys had all left her.

I kneel down in front of Umma and call her name. She smiles softly when I do, like she used to, but does not look at me. Her wrinkles are many now and her eyes are sunken. There is plenty of grey in her eyebrows and her lips are dry.

I hold her left hand and call her name again. She doesn't hold mine.

'I have returned, Umma,' I say. Slowly her fingers close into mine and she looks down at me. I gaze into her eyes to look for my mother, my Umma, who told me to behave well when I was leaving for Bayan Layi, who taught me the Arabic that saved me from a lot of beating. I cannot see her. Still holding my hand she looks up again. I cannot help it, I break down and sob.

'Umma, I am sorry,' I say, wiping the tears flowing from my eyes.

Khadija sits by her side, crying, asking if she will not at least say something to her son. There is a little smile on her face, but there is no Umma. This woman sitting here has her eyes, her smile, her dark circles but is not Umma. The Umma I know talks to me even when she is upset or worried, she talks to me even when she has to scold me, she talks to me.

'Sannu,' Umma finally says to me. One word! Hello. She gets up and goes back inside to lie down.

'Oh Allah, give her health,' Khadija cries, 'Allah, give her health.'

My legs are weak and my head hurts. Khadija takes the polythene bags inside and tells me to go and clean myself. The well in the house is full because of the rains and it is easy to fetch from. I take the metal bucket into the bathroom. The floor is muddy but there are two long planks on which I stand and place the bucket. The water is cold. Water from a well does not allow soap to lather, not like the tap water in Sokoto. In some ways it is good because I don't need to use as much water to take my bath. I wonder what I can do to help my mother, to make her see me, remember me, talk to me. Allah knows best. Allah knows best.

Khadija gives me an old torn mat to say maghrib prayers. She is glad I have brought some grains because they had run short and were wondering how they were going to make it until Friday, when the government has promised to distribute food in the area. Since the floods the villages have been getting weekly rations from the local government but last week they didn't get any. The trucks just didn't show up. Allah brought me at the right time, Khadija says. I wish I had come earlier, I tell her.

Khadija tells me all that has been happening: how the floods came and how my father died. He had lost the farm because he couldn't pay the rent on the land. He started complaining of headaches and one day he didn't come out for the early morning prayers. When Umma went in to check on him, his eyes were white and his body was cold.

Khadija is afraid for my brothers. She says they joined a Shiite group in Tashar Kanuri and came back acting strange. She is sure they were brainwashed to follow the group, because our father was not Shiite. He hated the Shiites and all their practices—they insulted the other companions of the Prophet apart from Ali. Only a kafir does that, turning the Quran upside down, following hadiths fabricated for their own sake, she swears. She cries when she says my brothers have left the path of wisdom and of Islam.

I insist on sleeping out in the zaure when Khadija wonders where I am going to sleep. There are only two rooms in the house and her husband sleeps alone in one of them.

'I am used to sleeping outdoors,' I tell her.

Shuaibu taps my legs.

'Why are you out here?' he asks.

I rub my eyes and take off the wrapper Khadija gave me to cover myself.

'Khadija,' he screams and walks into the house.

'Why did you leave him out here?' I hear him telling her inside.

'I am sorry, Maigida, he said he was OK out there and you weren't back yet so I didn't know what to do.'

'But you could have asked him to stay in my room.'

'I am sorry, I didn't know if you would have liked it that way.'

'I know we don't have room for him but he has made a long journey and at least should sleep well.'

'Forgive me, Maigida, for Allah's sake.'

He hisses and asks me to go in. I drag the mat into his little room, which is opposite hers, and lay the mat on the floor.

'He brought some millet and maize flour and we made you some tuwo,' she says.

'Allah is King! May Allah bless it,' he replies.

He doesn't say much to me when he enters the room except to ask if I have seen my mother and prays that Allah should forbid worse things. I want to tell him about Sheikh Jamal, who asked me to come back if my mother let me; now that my mother isn't talking or listening to anyone, I can't ask her permission. The room is dark and I don't realise he is sleeping, until he begins to snore loudly. I lie down and rest my head on my folded arms.

I can't sleep. I wish I had someone to talk to. If Banda was here, he would know exactly what to do, how to do it. The thought of Banda wrapped in a cloth and buried under sand makes it hard to breathe. I wonder if Allah will grant him aljanna or if he will go to hellfire. He did not always perform salat, or fast and he drank haram, but he was kind to me and to many people. Allah judges the intentions of the heart. Allah knows. Malam Junaidu used to say that while we are still in our mothers' bellies an angel of Allah is commanded to write our destinies—how long we will live and how we will live and whether we will enter hellfire or not. Sometimes I get confused. All I pray is that Allah forgives him.

There is no adhan from a loudspeaker to wake me up and remind me that prayer is better than sleep. This is my favourite part of the early morning call to prayer:

As-salatu Khayrun Minan-nawm.

Prayer is better than sleep.

It is Khadija's husband who wakes me and gives me a little plastic kettle. The water in it is very cold because it was outside overnight. I close my eyes as I pour the water first over my face and grit my teeth as I feel a chill run from my head through my body. I do my ablution quickly, in front of Shuaibu's room and run after him as he heads out to the mosque, which is just a few houses away.

The breeze blows strong and cold in the mosque. It is just a square patch of land bounded by stones. I wonder why the Imam is in such a rush. The prayer is over very quickly and the men begin to talk about the flood and the government supplies that haven't come in two weeks. Some whose houses were destroyed have had to go to a camp set up by some foreigners for those affected by the flood to get food and drinking water. The food needs to get to those still remaining in the village, the Imam says, and he asks for volunteers to go and complain in the local government office. Four men volunteer and the Imam tells them to meet him in one hour at the mosque.

On our way back I speak to Khadija's husband.

'I told my malam I will return soon,' I lie.

'Who is your malam?' he asks.

'Sheikh Jamal,' I reply, afraid he might know him.

'Oh, the one at the motor park in the city. He is a good man, I know many people who have studied under him. Only be sure to return to see your mother often.'

'He asked me to get permission from my mother. I don't know how to do that.'

'Ah, you see, he is a good man. Not like the ones your brothers have decided to follow. They think they are grown men now and can do as they please. Nobody in their right senses follows the Shiites. But Allah knows, I have done what I can, I have spoken to them. They will regret their decision.'

I want him to tell me what to do but he is going on about my brothers and things I don't want to hear. Just say to me go, or don't go! I won't ask again. Even if Umma doesn't hear me I will tell her I want to leave. Allah knows my intentions. Insha Allah, when I come back she will see me. One day, insha Allah, I will take her out of this place to the city, where there are hospitals and bright fluorescent lights.

PART TWO

Back to Sokoto

2006

Every time I stop to think that I have been happy these past few years in Sokoto, I kill the thought in my head because I am afraid that my being happy will jinx it. I have learned to tell lies to escape bad memories that come from telling my stories. It all started when I first came back. I did not say when Sheikh Jamal asked how my mother was that when I held her hand and told her I was leaving she didn't even look at me; that she preferred to look up at the sky or to the ground than give me her blessings or advise me to be good in Sokoto. I didn't tell him that every time I have returned to Dogon Icce for the Sallah celebrations I have found Umma looking more sickly and pale, that her fingers are bruised and bloody from her chewing on them, that her hair has turned grey and her skin is wrinkled, that Khadija feeds her like a little baby because she never eats and that they have now had to chain her to the bed in the room because many times she has gone missing, been found wandering aimlessly without a scarf or hijab in the village. I haven't told him how Khadija suffers alone with her daughter and Umma because her husband has abandoned her and built a little hut nearby where he lives with his new wife—the last daughter of the village imam. The girl has a son and is pregnant with another child. Every month, he sends Khadija some grain and once in a long while a little money, barely enough for a pot of soup. He has refused to divorce her and set her free, yet he does not want to keep her.

I just tell Sheikh that all is well in the village and try all I can to take grain and soap when I go. Khadija thinks that Shuaibu married another wife because he was tired of her spending so much time taking care of Umma. She says that nothing will make her stop and that after all, taking another wife is sunna for him. I feel guilty and grateful all at the same time. She shouldn't have to choose between Umma and her husband.

I found, when I first returned, that Sheikh was not only the imam but also a member of the committee that is in charge of running the mosque. The mosque committee is responsible for choosing the imam and his deputy and raising funds. Sheikh is the vice-chairman while Alhaji Usman, who is rarely around because he travels so much, is the chairman. Alhaji Usman built the mosque and still sends food for sadaka many Fridays. The three very old men who always pray in front, Malam Yunusa, Malam Abduljalal and Malam Hamza, are on the committee too. Malam Hamza is often ill and hardly ever around. Malam Abdul-Nur is not on the committee. A lot of people pray at this mosque and I have heard some people talk of expanding it. The land to the right of the mosque was also donated by Alhaji Usman. I wonder how much money he has, because it is hard to tell from the way he dresses. He wears the same type of white caftans that Sheikh and Malam Abdul-Nur wear. He does not wear gold teeth to show he has been to Mecca even though I hear he has been there many times. He has even performed the hajj on behalf of his sick parents, who couldn't travel.

Sometimes it is good to be invisible, to just go around the park doing my own thing and helping out in the mosque without anyone noticing me. Also I don't have to share any stories that will put me in trouble. When one talks too much, one exposes oneself. I remember a boy who would not stop talking and told everyone about robbing and injuring a policeman whose cousin was one of the men listening. The boy is still in prison.

I don't like sitting with the boys around the mosque or the motor park because all they do is talk about whose penis is big and whose penis is small and whose penis is curved like a fishing hook. And every time Abdulkareem is around everyone jokes about how he has to fold his penis three times before it can fit in his pants. I wondered how everyone knew what his penis looked like. Then someone told me that there was a time some boys wanted to see it when the rumours started going round. When Abdulkareem refused to show them, they all pinned and held him down, stripped him and stroked his penis until it became like a big fat sugar cane. Some people say it is a sickness to have such a big penis. I have never seen it. I do not want to see it.

Abdulkareem and Bilal, who, like me, used to sleep in the same little room behind the mosque, have both gone to Kebbi to work for Alhaji Usman's brother, who owns a large fish farm. Somehow I think Sheikh was happy to let them go. I am glad they have gone. They talked very loud and played very rough, like little children. Abdulkareem was a tall, fair boy with a lot of hair on his legs, hands and chest, whose father, mother and brothers had been killed in one of the riots in Jos. He had returned from the next village to find the burnt corpses of his family in front of the house. I am not sure of Bilal's story because he used to tell a different story every time. First he told me he ran away from his home in Minna because his father was wicked and didn't give him food. Then he said his father was fighting infidel Americans in Afghanistan, then he said Iraq, then both. His father has been both dead and alive, in Nigeria and out of Nigeria, a wicked man and a brave fighter. One of Bilal's eyes is half shut and has a scar above it. He had many stories for that too. He said once that he was looking up at a plane when some object fell from it and hit him in the eye. Then he said he got the injury fighting off four armed policemen with his bare hands. He was going to be a soldier if not for his eye. Bilal spoke fast and even though most people knew he was lying, they enjoyed the stories. I found that it was useless to contradict Bilal. He would quickly create an excuse for any discrepancy and patch up his story.

Bilal and Abdulkareem were always coming out of corners or disappearing together. When they would reappear they would both be quiet for a long time and I would suspect they were up to no good. For a long time I tried to find out where they always went and what they were doing. At first I was sure that they were smoking something. So I would come very close to them to see if I could smell anything. I tried this a few times, but apart from the occasional mouth and body odour I would smell nothing. Sometimes one of them would smell like raw yams that had just been peeled.

There were two new toilets built behind the mosque and I was thrilled to be using a flush toilet for the first time in my life. In some ways it was similar to the pit toilet I was used to—we still squatted—only now, you could see your shit after you finished and it only disappeared after you pulled the rope connected to the flush handle on the water tank above. We also bathed there. Sometimes I forgot to pull the handle on the water tank, until I had gone out of the toilet. Then I would come running back to pull the handle. I liked the sound of the water as it ran down the pipe and into the toilet, making it white again. Abdulkareem and Bilal took turns to clean the toilet twice a day, while I organised the boys who swept the mosque. Many people didn't care about pulling the handle to flush the toilet; they just went in and did their business. When someone was caught he would complain that there was no water in the tank. But there were also buckets and a well outside the toilet. Eventually we decided to lock one of the toilets, which only Sheikh and Malam Abdul-Nur or their visitors used. That one was always clean.

I feel relieved that I don't have to see Bilal and Abdulkareem anymore because of what I saw one day. They had both disappeared as usual and I wasn't thinking anything of it. I had given up trying to find out what they were up to. I woke up in the middle of the night needing to pee badly and ran into the toilet without knocking. There was no electricity and I had my little torch with me. As I opened the door, loosening the rope of my trousers, someone almost knocked me over and ran out. I turned and from the back of his head I recognised him as Bilal. He wasn't wearing a shirt and was clutching at his trousers like they were going to fall. I flashed my torch in the toilet and saw Abdulkareem standing there, struggling to pull up his trousers and wipe his hands at the same time. His penis was huge and erect and he was panting like he had been running.

'Stop flashing that light on me!' he screamed.

Suddenly the urge to pee disappeared and I shut the door. Only Bilal came back that night and I pretended I was asleep. I don't know where Abdulkareem slept, or if he slept at all that night. I knew that even though I had caught them, Bilal would try to lie his way out of it. Malam Junaidu said it was a sin fasting could not cleanse. I had heard of men being together, read many hadiths about sodomy, but I had never seen it with my own eyes. I wondered what they did before I came and how they did it. When I imagined how painful it was sometimes to shit in the toilet, especially when I ate a lot of bread, I wondered if Bilal didn't feel pain allowing Abdulkareem's penis inside him. I thought of the hadith that said that the earth trembles whenever there is an act of sodomy and wondered how many times they had done it and if I ever felt the earth tremble. It made me feel nauseated when I thought of it—Abdulkareem touching Bilal, Bilal bending over—how they could prefer themselves to girls? And there were many bad girls in the park if they wanted, girls who used to go into the backseats of empty buses at night and let men touch them. Sheikh used to say he would send away all those drivers from the park if he could and stop girls from coming in at night. He once spoke to the head of the motor park union, who said he would talk to the drivers, but nothing changed.

The morning after, I waited for them to beg me not to say anything and when they didn't I was angry and wanted to tell Sheikh. But I couldn't and found it hard to sleep with them in the room. The room was quiet for many nights. I resented them because they could sleep, and it was I who stayed up with thoughts plaguing my mind. Then one night, when I was finally able to sleep, I dreamt I was out in the bush with Abdulkareem and he pinned me against a tree and made me bend over and forced his huge penis into me. The penis wouldn't enter and I begged him to stop. But he kept pushing and pushing and laughing. I woke up with my penis erect and sweat all over my body.

It came as a blessing when not long after, they both left for Kebbi to work on the fish farm. After a few weeks, it wasn't so strong in my mind anymore—I stopped thinking of them and being irritated every time I went to use the toilet or take my bath and I was able to sleep. I didn't mind that I had to clean the toilets as well as check on the boys sweeping the mosque; I was just glad that they were gone.

I miss my Umma. Especially in the morning after fajr prayers when I have nothing to do. It feels strange not having a father and having a mother who can't talk to you; it makes me feel alone and cold like standing without clothes in the rain. When I want to scream and cry I hear Sheikh Jamal's voice in my head: Allah knows why. Allah knows why.

Sheikh is kind. He is different from Malam Junaidu in Bayan Layi, who made us beg even after working on his maize farm. Working on a farm during planting and harvest season is better than standing by the road, chasing after cars and having people turn away from you like you are a huge mound of shit. It is better than fighting over food and money at the Friday mosque.

It feels like a faraway dream sometimes—leaving Bayan Layi, escaping the hunger, sleeping outdoors during the rains and harmattan . . . and the police guns that last day! I still hear the rat-tat-tat, the screaming, the smoke; still see the boys trying to dodge the bullets; still see Banda, coughing, telling me to run as he doubled over from pain in his chest . . . I still feel it—the feeling of a tight string that has snapped in my chest, when I saw him finally fall flat. These are the things I wish I could tell my Umma. Only her, because only my mother would understand that I didn't mean to do those bad things for the Small Party people during the elections; that when I struck the fat Big Party man, it was because I was angry and afraid; that in my heart I wished Tsohon Soja, who stood guard outside the Big Party office, hadn't been so stubborn. Then we would have just burnt the office and let him go.

Astaghfirullah, but I find myself still wishing Abdulkareem and Bilal would fall inside a well of soldier ants that will eat them up slowly. I hate them because even though I thought it was all gone, I still have these dreams. I hate them more because the dreams seem to go on forever and I wake up with my penis hard. I am afraid to lie face down when it is very hard because it hurts a bit and I wonder if it can break.

I cannot tell Sheikh about these dreams because I will have to tell him what happened. What if he thinks that I also like it because I am having dreams? What makes it worse is the way everything makes my penis hard these days.

Yesterday I cried. I cried because when Malam Abdul-Nur put his hand on my shoulder to tell me he liked the way I always got up early to take care of the mosque, I felt it again.

The flashes from that dream; the flashes that make me go to a quiet corner to hide my erection. He touched me and it all came rushing through my head: Abdulkareem, his wicked grin, holding my waist, refusing to stop even though he could see it wouldn't enter. I wanted to go away when it started, but Malam Abdul-Nur decided this was the time to give me a long sermon about not joining the motor park boys who smoke cigarettes under the mango trees at night. He has never seen me smoke or sit with the boys who smoke and, wallahi, since I left the boys under the kuka tree in Bayan Layi, my mouth has not touched a cigarette. The feeling was worse than what I feel when I need to shit and there is someone in the toilet—you have to walk over five minutes to reach the nearest bush outside the motor park. When he finally finished his speech and let go of my shoulder, I walked away quickly. I felt dirty as I sat on the far edge of the culvert near the taps in front of the mosque. I struggled to block out all the images flying through my head: good thoughts clashing with bad thoughts clashing with guilty thoughts, chasing each other until I felt dizzy. My balls felt swollen and painful. I wished I could just cut off the whole damn thing. Allah forgive my thoughts, but I wondered at that moment why Allah put this thing in our bodies; I wished I was a woman. I went into the toilet and locked the door. Then, I brought it out. I didn't want to. I tried hard not to, but the feeling was strong and raging in my body like the fast running water in a river during the rainy season. At first I just held it. Afterwards I shut my eyes and stroked it, slowly, then quickly until a feverish cold passed all over my body and gripped me and made my legs wobbly and I needed to use my left hand to support myself against the wall. When it passed, I had made a mess of the toilet floor, my hands and my trousers. I peeped through the space in the door to make sure no one was waiting to use the toilet. Then I rushed to get a bucket of water to take my bath and cleanse myself. As I poured the water over my head, I cried. And hated that I enjoyed it so much.

Fighting

Wai wai wai!
Ba da jimawa ba sai Lahira ta yi bako . . .
Ba mu dogara ga laya
Ba mu dogara ga tsafi . . .

Wai wai wai!
Just a little while and the Hereafter will receive a
guest . . .
We place no reliance on amulets
We place no reliance on charms . . .

A short, muscular fighter, wearing only tight brown shorts, stands with his legs spread apart, chanting before the start of a dambe match. Opposite him, in the centre of the sandy ring around which spectators sit, his tall and bulky opponent stands. Another man sprays water from his mouth onto the naked torso of the tall fighter. With the exception of the short man, who everyone knows as Aminu Hogan, all of the others have amulets around their arms and one fist wrapped in pieces of cloth and bound with rope. As the referee who is holding a whip asks them to begin, the cheering crowd goes quiet. They both crouch, watching, looking for a weakness, for the right time to land a punch. In the background drummers provide accompaniment to three singers. Hogan tilts his body to the right with his gloved right hand swinging below and his left hand up in the air, shielding him. The tall fighter, Labo Kato, looks more self-assured and seems like he is just waiting to win the match and return to something more important.

Labo attempts to lunge forward but is repelled by Hogan's left hand. He tries again, and almost trips as Hogan dodges and gives way. The crowd sighs with relief. As Labo tries to regain his balance, Hogan leaps into the air and sinks his right fist into Labo's jaw. Like a sack of beans he goes down, his eyes half shut. The audience screams and the drummers become even more animated as the match comes to a premature end. People applaud and chant: A-mi-nu! Ho-gan!

Hogan chants, prancing about, waving his right hand in the air:

Ba mu dogara ga laya
Ba mu dogara ga tsafi . . .

I need to pee before the next match. Outside the empty, fenced-in field, which is used for dambe, people are selling cigarettes, pure water and soft drinks. I go out behind the wall, away from the people chatting in groups. As I squat, I notice three Keke Napeps parked not far away to my right. The tricycle in the middle rocks gently. I move closer and hear the sound of a girl suppressing a scream. I listen again and realise her cries are not of pain. After a few seconds a man pokes his head out from the Keke and sees me. He hurries out adjusting his trousers and runs off, away from the fence. The girl follows after him a few seconds later.

As I walk back to the dambe arena I pass by a 'dan daudu leaning on the fence speaking to another man. I know he is a 'dan daudu because of all the tozali around his eyes and his voice, which sounds like that of a woman, and the way he is clapping and twirling his hands like a woman and the scarf, which sits lazily on his head.

'Alhaji, I hear you are very demanding,' the 'dan daudu says to the man, 'don't worry I have your exact match. If you say yes I will send her to you later. But this one costs more fa. You know how sweet soup costs money.'

The man laughs, dragging on his cigarette. 'OK, send. Let her just not complain.'

'Yes, can I help you?' the 'dan daudu shouts to me when he notices I am staring. I walk away quickly.

Sheikh's voice keeps me from enjoying this dambe. Instead of going back in I walk past the gate in the direction of the main road that leads to the mosque. I hear his voice in my head calling the dambe ground the house of Shaitan, where all sorts of kufr and haram are enjoyed. This is the second time I have been here and I feel ashamed of myself, of allowing the cheering to attract me to this place we have all been warned about. I hope no one from the mosque saw me go in there. I do not like this guilt and hiding and feeling like a kafir. I will not come back.

Jibril

Sheikh has a lot of books in his office. I have read them all except the ones in English and the unopened ones in the cartons. He gets a lot of books as gifts, many even from outside Nigeria. It's a shame I can't read the ones in English. Sometimes when I don't understand the Arabic words or know their meaning I just memorise them and ask Sheikh later. I have a small Arabic to Hausa dictionary which I used until I memorised all the words in the dictionary and knew their meanings. Sheikh has a bigger dictionary but it is an Arabic to English dictionary. I want to learn English.

Each time Malam Abdul-Nur or Sheikh speak on the phone in English, I get lost listening to them. It sounds soft and easy like one does not need to open one's mouth a lot or use a lot of air or energy. With Arabic one uses everything, the neck, the jaws, the tongue. Especially the throat. I don't think the words touch the throat when you speak English. It just comes out with the air.

Sheikh must have many more books in his house. Many times I wonder how his house looks on the inside. Not many people I know have been there. Everyone claims they have been, but when I ask specific questions it becomes clear that they are lying. The rumours are that his first daughter, Aisha, who hardly ever leaves the house, is very beautiful. I have never seen her before so I cannot judge for myself. Sheikh doesn't like people from the mosque going to his house. Only those who are very close to him like Malam Abdul-Nur know the house well.

There is a boy in a tight yellow T-shirt standing outside the mosque in plastic sandals with two yellow-and-black striped polythene bags on the ground between his feet. He is staring at the mosque. His mouth is bunched and his nose widened like someone who has been punched just before a fight is forcibly broken up. His cheeks are bony and his forehead is lumpy and he has scars, like someone who has been in a lot of street fights. It is easy to tell from his knuckles that he has wounded himself a lot from punching people in the mouth. He is about the same size as me.

Malam Abdul-Nur peeps from the mosque and motions to the boy to come in. He hesitates. Malam Abdul-Nur then shouts something in a language I don't know. The boy slowly picks up his bags and walks towards us, frowning.

Right in front of the mosque the boy stops again. Malam Abdul-Nur grabs him by the hand and drags him inside. They walk into Sheikh's office and shut the door. I go back into the mosque, curious. I pick up a broom and sweep, climb a stool to remove cobwebs—every excuse to come closer to the office and hear what is being said. I hear nothing.

They are in the office for about an hour. Malam Abdul-Nur emerges first from the office followed by the boy and then Sheikh. I pretend to continue sweeping.

'Ahmad. We have a guest. His name is Jibril.'

'Gabriel!' The boy interrupts Sheikh.

Malam Abdul-Nur glowers at the boy and reaches to slap him. Sheikh restrains him.

'He is Malam Abdul-Nur's brother. From Ilorin. He will stay with you in the back room. Pull out a mattress from the store for him.'

I drop the broom and head to the room behind the mosque. I move my little radio, my bag which Sheikh gave to me and the photo of Sheikh Inyass I found one day on the ground at the motor park. The photo of Sheikh Inyass is identical to the one Umma had in her room in Dogon Icce. I unroll the mattress Abdulkareem and Bilal shared when they were here, lay it on the right side of the room and cover it with the only other bedsheet. I am thinking as I move things around whether to call him Jibril or Gabriel.

He opens the door and drops his bags by his feet. I stretch out my right hand. He is still frowning and looking around the room. He shakes my hand but lets go almost immediately.

He doesn't unpack. He doesn't relax. He doesn't stop frowning and bunching his lips. I see the horizontal scar that runs from the side of his mouth right across the right half of his upper lip and I think of Gobedanisa and the scar that Banda gave him. Suddenly I want to tell him my stories of Bayan Layi that I have not told anyone, so he can tell me his own stories of how he got his scars and where he comes from.

I want to say something but my mouth won't open. It is like waking up in the night from a bad dream and I cannot scream or get up or move any part of my body because it feels like someone is pressing me down. I am always scared when that happens.

I can't sleep. I roll over and find the boy restless and slapping his body to fight mosquitoes. The ceiling fan is off because the noise it makes in my ear is like bottle tops being scraped over concrete. But it keeps away the mosquitoes. I turn it on and give him one of the cloths I use to cover myself. He looks up with his puffy eyes and takes it from me.

The ceiling fan is grating away and the boy has started snoring. The combination of the two noises creates a sound like a song—not as bad as just the ceiling fan alone. Like groundnuts and tiger nuts. Eating groundnuts alone makes my chest burn but together with tiger nuts they are nice and taste like milk that has a bit of salt in it.

Many memories float in my head. Memories of when all of my family was still in one house in Dogon Icce. When Maccido used to pinch me and I would cry and nobody would believe me when I would say what he did. When I used to be angry that the twins got anything they wanted and my father hit Umma, Maccido and me, but never them. When I heard Umma screaming and the midwife who came to help her give birth came out with a bag that my father eventually went to bury. When the midwife came again after less than a year and my father had to make that trip to the burial ground a second time. When in Bayan Layi, Malam Junaidu flogged a boy who couldn't remember his Quranic verses with his tyre whip and the boy threw up blood, was taken away and never came back.

The memories dance around in my head like my image dances around when I look at myself in a pool of water that isn't still.

Sheikh comes into the room himself, waking us up earlier than usual. It is Thursday and like him we fast on Mondays and Thursdays. He has brought in hot koko, kosai, some bread, dates and slices of watermelon and pineapples. I am wondering what the occasion is. Usually this type of feasting is reserved for Ramadan. He squats to sit with us on the mat between my flat mattress and that of the other boy. I get up.

'Sit, sit,' he says.

The other boy scratches his red eyes. He looks at the food spread out before us like he was going to jump into the plates. Yesterday he refused to eat or drink.

Sheikh speaks to the boy kindly, in English. I don't know what Sheikh says but by the time he switches to Hausa, the boy is looking down like someone who has done something wrong. I hate the fact that I do not understand what has just been said.

'Please, let us eat,' Sheikh says to both of us.

I am surprised that Sheikh has even brought bowls with water for us to wash our hands in. Reluctantly, like a child receiving a gift from a stranger, the boy washes his hands and joins us. I am too shy to eat in front of Sheikh. He fills up the room and it is hard to breathe. He has never spent so much time here before.

'This fan needs repairs,' he says, 'it shouldn't make so much noise. Please remind me, Ahmad. There is someone coming to fix the one in my house tomorrow. He will fix this one too.'

He stares at the photo of Sheikh Inyass by my bed. I tell him it is mine when he asks. He eats some more before he starts speaking again.

'Have you ever heard of shirk? Do you know what it is?'

'Yes ya Sheikh,' I reply, 'it is joining of any other thing with Allah subhanahu wa ta'ala.'

'Interesting. And is that a good or bad thing?'

'A horrible thing, ya Sheikh.'

'And bid'a?'

'Creating new things that are not in the Quran or Sunna.'

'Good?'

'Horrible, ya Sheikh.'

'Do we make photos of Allah subhanahu wa ta'ala?'

'Never, ya Sheikh. Never.'

'What of photos of his Prophet sallallahu alaihi wasallam?'

'No.'

'Do you know of the one thing that Allah subhanahu wa ta'ala will not forgive?'

I remember the answer from Quranic school, and from my father when he used to speak against Shiites:

Innallaha la yaghfiru an yushraka bihi wayagfiru ma duna zalika liman yasha'u waman yushrik billahi faqad iftara ith-man 'aadheeman.

Allah forgives not that partners should be set up with Him, but He forgives anything else, to whom He pleases; to set up partners with Allah is to devise a sin most heinous indeed.

I feel ashamed. I remove the photo from the side of the bed, fold it and stuff it in my bag. Sheikh's gaze upon me is heavy. He is smiling and I can feel his eyes looking through my head and my chest for the things I am feeling and thinking. Suddenly, the food is hard to swallow and the koko is tasteless in my mouth.

Sheikh gulps down what is left of the water in his steel cup and rises to his feet. He turns to the boy and asks if he would like to go for a stroll after the morning prayers. He says it like a question but it is not really a question. It is the kind of question that tells you exactly what to do, in such a way that you cannot refuse or complain.

Pictures don't excite me the way they excite other boys. When they see a poster or a picture from an old magazine used to wrap kosai they gather round, pointing and laughing and staring as if their stomachs would become full by looking at it. Some of them collect bubble gum wrappers that have photos and show off when they have more than others. Pictures make me remember. There are many things I want to hide away in my head. I imagine that when you have a picture, the things become permanent and you can never remove the thought from your head. But sometimes I want to remember. It is why I keep this photo of Sheikh Inyass. I see it and the walls of Umma's room come back to me, when she still had words in her mouth and life in her eyes. That is the only memory I want.

I have just prayed asr. I climb onto the heap of rubbish outside the motor park and let the folded photo of Sheikh Inyass fall from my hand without looking. If I see where the paper lands I might be tempted to come back for it before the rubbish heap is set ablaze. It will be gone by evening.

The new boy is sitting on the left side of the low outer fence of the mosque, swinging his legs and playing with a long dry stick. He greets me with his eyes and continues striking the ground with his stick.

'Have you eaten?' I ask him.

'Yes,' he says, 'inside the big office.'

I feel a little jealous. Sheikh has never offered me food inside his office before. I wonder what Sheikh has been telling him all day while they have been together. As I turn to leave, I ask him what his name is so I don't offend him by calling him something he doesn't want.

'Gabriel,' he says.

'But you can call me Jibril.'

He looks away. I look away, and walk towards our room.

PART THREE

Words

2009

Jibril is the fastest person I know. He finishes his food, washes and puts away his plates when I am barely halfway through mine. When we have to do laundry for Malam Abdul-Nur and Sheikh and we split the clothes into two equal piles, he finishes washing, rinsing and hanging long before me and even sometimes offers to help with mine. The same with ironing. In the three years that he has been here, he has learned how to read Arabic and everyone says his pronunciation is better than his brother's. At first I taught him Arabic with the agreement that he would teach me English. Now I have nothing to teach him because he has learned everything I know and has read everything I have read. But I still struggle with English—he still corrects me every other day. It is frustrating, but he doesn't get tired, even if he has to explain things to me over and over again.

When Jibril first came, he stared away for long moments, avoiding my eyes. He looked like he was both angry and afraid. He reminded me of when I first went to Malam Junaidu's school—how it was all strange and everyone looked like they did not like me. I did not like them. I did not like the way they all stared at me and made me seem like I did not belong there. Like I was there to take something from them. So I tried not to look at him too much and make him uncomfortable and let him stare away and be angry and afraid, because I knew that it would pass. I knew that if you stare enough at something new, your eyes get used to it and it is not scary or strange anymore. He pretended not to be interested when I started telling him of the first time I came to Malam Junaidu but by the time I had finished telling about all the boys there, he was nodding and smiling and laughing.

I don't like the way Jibril returns with a red eye or swollen lip many times after his brother has sent for him. Jibril is too old to be beaten like a child. I don't like the way Malam Abdul-Nur hits people, especially the new boys, who have started living in the newly built rooms by the side of ours behind the mosque. Apart from me, the only people who live in the mosque he does not hit are Umar, Sambo and Mohammed, who act as Sheikh's bodyguards. Last month he whipped one of the boys, Khalil, with a horsewhip until he bled and Chuks had to treat his wounds. Jibril too has whip marks all over his back. He tells me most of them were from home in Ilorin, where their uncle used to beat all the children in his house every Friday, just in case they had done something he didn't know of during the week.

*   *   *

Last month Malam Abdul-Nur stopped me at the entrance
of the mosque and asked me if there was anything I wanted.
First I was confused, thinking that perhaps he wanted to
scold me for having done something wrong. But then his
eyes were relaxed and the lines of his forehead weren't so
many and he wasn't breathing hard like he does when he is
upset. Reluctantly I told him I wanted a radio that has stations outside Nigeria—something like the big one in Sheikh's
office, but smaller, so that I can carry it around. At some
point it crossed my mind that perhaps he wanted me to do
something for him.

A few days after, he sent for me. He had just moved into
his own office at the back of the mosque not far from where
our rooms were. The new office has white walls and tiles and a
small toilet inside. Since Sheikh has decided to make Malam
Abdul-Nur the headmaster of the new school that is to be
built on the land adjacent to the mosque, the office will also
be the office of the headmaster. I wonder about toilets that
are built inside rooms. Will the whole room not smell when
someone uses the toilet?

The office has a ceiling fan and a standing fan. The
curtains in the office are not the normal type hanging from
a rope nailed into the wall. They close and open when you
pull a rope that has tiny plastic balls like a small chasbi.
Alhaji Usman's workmen built the office and they finished
the construction and painting in only three weeks. The same
men will build the school.

I chewed on my nails as Malam Abdul-Nur picked up
two small cartons from under his table and made some notes
in his exercise book. I could not read what he wrote because

it was upside down from where I was sitting, but I could see that he was writing in Arabic.

Malam Abdul-Nur did not raise his head from his exercise book when he asked: 'If Allah asks you to do something, will you refuse?'

When I did not answer, he stopped writing, dropped his pen slowly and massaged his eyeballs. Then he looked at me.

'No,' I said, confused.

'Are you just saying it, or do you understand it, what it means to do what Allah wants without any question?'

'I don't understand.'

'Are you ready to do what Allah wants when He wants it, without asking why?'

'Yes.'

'Yes. I know you will.'

He pointed at the two cartons.

'Your radio is in the bigger carton. And because of how well-behaved you have been since you came here—I have been watching you; I see everybody, those who are bad and those who are good and those who are just here eating our food—the smaller carton is also for you.'

'Thank you, Malam.'

'Will you be able to use the phone or do you want me to show you how to set it up?'

'Let me try, Malam.'

'If you have any issues let me know.'

In my heart I should have been happy but I was not. I have a funny feeling about Malam Abdul-Nur, Allah forgive me. It is hard to describe. It is a little bit of fear, a little bit of anger that he doesn't want Jibril to talk to me and a little bit of confusion because I don't know what is going on in his mind. I cannot say that he is kind because he slaps people when he is angry. I cannot say that he is wicked because he also gives people gifts. And Allah only judges what is inside a person's heart.

I came back into the room and saw Jibril opening a small carton just like mine. He got a phone too. I watched how he opened it and put the SIM card inside it. Then I did the same with mine.

Tuning the radio to find stations, I find BBC Hausa and BBC English. I like BBC Hausa. Especially the news. It is surprising that I learn new Hausa words from a foreign radio station. Comparing the news on BBC English to that on BBC Hausa is interesting. Sometimes I do not know a word in English and I hear it in Hausa and I understand. Other times there is a Hausa phrase I have never heard before, like Majalisar Dinkin Duniya, which BBC English calls United Nations. If I had not heard the English, I would have translated it to mean 'Association of Joining the World.' But then if I had heard United Nations I would have called it Dinkakun Kasashe in Hausa. Words turn into something else when they change from Hausa to English and back.

Sheikh has been planning a fundraising campaign and launch for the new school. We sent lots of invitations out and we expect the local government chairman to come. Alhaji Usman has already pledged to give most of the money once the plans are ready.

A group of five men from England came to visit Sheikh recently and only one of them was white. The rest of them were black and had names like us. The difference was the way they spoke English, just like the people on BBC English. And they spoke Arabic too. It was exciting. I do not know much about this, but I think I prefer England to America. Or maybe it is that I don't like America at all. I did not realise there were black people and even Arabs who call England their country. They don't just live there—they call it their own, just like the white people.

Malam Abdul-Nur raised his hand when one of the men from England had finished speaking. The man had said that Islam means peace and that all Muslims should be examples of peace in the community. Malam Abdul-Nur said he wanted to make a correction.

'Islam does not mean peace,' he began. All of us went quiet in the room apart from the boys who follow him everywhere he goes and shout Allahu Akbar after everything he says. They are very annoying, those boys.

The way he spoke English, I did not believe it was Malam Abdul-Nur speaking. I was taking notes so that I could find out later from Jibril any words I did not understand. Malam Abdul-Nur's voice was different. He sounded almost like the men from England, as if there was a small man inside him pushing the words out through his nose.

'Islam means submission. Submission to the will of Allah. And the will of Allah is not the will of the infidel or the will of America. Islam means that we do not submit to anything or anyone but Allah.'

It is not that I do not agree with Malam Abdul-Nur. It was the way he tried to make them look like they did not know what they were saying. We all understood what they were saying. They were telling us to be good and kind to change the way the world sees us Muslims. One of the men said that after the planes entered the tall buildings in America and killed people, many people started talking of Islam as if all Muslims were bombers or terrorists. He said that we must change the way people think of our religion and always ask ourselves if anything we are doing will give Islam a good or bad name.

When Sheikh finished thanking the men for coming all the way from England to see the Muslims in Nigeria and for coming to our small mosque, he spoke about the launch of the new Quranic school and the Jama'atul Ihyau Islamil Haqiqiy—the Society for the Restoration of True Islam. I think the five men were happy with this because they all dropped something, fisabilillah, in the boxes on their way out. I wonder how Sheikh met them.

When everybody had left, Malam Abdul-Nur asked me to help count the money in the boxes. When we counted the last box he told me I could leave. I thought that I would help with adding everything together. I kept all the numbers in my head. In all, we had eighty two thousand six hundred ninety naira. So I was surprised when Sheikh was talking later in the evening about how good their visit was, how full the mosque was and how people dropped 'as much as seventy thousand naira' in the boxes. I thought it was a mistake but Malam Abdul-Nur was nodding in agreement. I don't forget numbers.

I don't understand why Sheikh and Malam Abdul-Nur are together. They are so different.

The other day, Jibril was teaching me how to use 'him' and 'her' in English. It was confusing. He said: 'Give her her book' and asked me to make the same sentence with 'him.' I knew it was 'Give him his book.' But I didn't understand why.

'Why is it not "Give him him book," simple, like in Hausa?' I asked. 'That's just how it is,' he said. 'English is a foolish language,' I replied. He laughed and said we should see who could remember the most words from the list we had made of words that end with tion. I knew he would win and was just trying to show off. I get confused with tion. Some words end with sion but they are pronounced the same. Many times I think I can never really understand this language. The one thing I know I will never ever get is when to use its and it's. I think I know the difference but Jibril always says I get it wrong when I write.

We kept going, shouting the words at each other, giggling. He laughed at my pronunciations. Neither of us realised that Malam Abdul-Nur was standing by the entrance, watching. Jibril was the first to notice him because he was facing the door. I saw his face change. He stopped saying the words and I turned around. Malam Abdul-Nur said something to him in Yoruba and walked away. Jibril closed his notebook and told me he would be back soon. I felt bad and hoped that he would just be scolded and not beaten.

Very soon I will have memorised all the words in my book. When I find a word in an English book I do not know, I underline it and write it out. I check the meaning in Jibril's little dictionary. Sometimes I don't understand the definition and he has to explain it to me. I like the way Jibril explains things.

'Oh this one, it is very easy,' he often says.

Then he uses a thing you know to explain the word, giving you plenty of examples and asking you questions until you understand it. Malam Abdul-Nur on the other hand is very impatient and insults you if you do not understand the first time, calling you dakiki, dull, stupid. Once, Jibril explained the word 'illogical' to me. We had read it in a page from a colourful magazine that was used to wrap kosai that we bought from

Saudatu, the older woman who also sells koko in the motor park. He first confessed he didn't really know the word and looked it up in the dictionary, then read the sentence again. The definition was just 'without logic' and we had to check what 'logic' meant. He was not satisfied and we went to Sheikh's office to use the large dictionary, which has better definitions and uses the words in sentences. I hate it when a dictionary defines one word with another word I do not know. Then I get lost because I end up looking at other words that interest me and forget what word I was looking for in the first place.

I love learning new words. I love reading the definitions and examples in Sheikh's dictionary, then finding those words in books or magazines and using the words with the only person who can get them, Jibril. Occasionally I find somebody in the park I can speak English with. People are always surprised when I speak English.

I have bought a bigger hardcover notebook and started using the words I like in sentences, explaining them using examples like Jibril does. When this book is full, I think I will have learned enough to teach English.

I feel terrible about what happened yesterday. I could not find Jibril, and his phone was saying it was switched off. I was sure that he had run away like he always said he would because of how often his brother beats him. Sheikh came into our room as I was outside with the others clearing the gutters around the mosque. He found a book with the picture of a naked woman on it called *Every Woman* lying on my mattress. Someone had left it in one of Sheikh's buses and hadn't come back for it for months. So I decided to take it and keep it. When he asked me what I was doing with it, Allah forgive me,

I lied and said that I had never touched the book before and did not know what it was about. I told him it was Jibril who owned the book. Sheikh did not say anything. He just took the book away. Then just before prayers in the evening I saw Jibril come down from one of the buses with clothes in his hand. Malam Abdul-Nur had sent him to the tailor and told him to stay there until the tailor finished everything. Thinking of it again, it was stupid for me to think he had run away because all his clothes were there and his phone charger was still in the socket.

After the late evening prayers Jibril was with Malam Abdul-Nur for a long time. I could not sit or eat or sleep. My mouth was bitter and my stomach felt as dirty as the gutters we cleaned.

When Jibril came in afterwards, he took off his shirt. He did not say a word. When he turned and I saw the new wounds on his back, tears began to roll down my eyes. I knelt down and begged him.

'I thought you had run away Jibril!'

Still, he did not say anything. But there was no anger on his face or in his eyes. He just sat on the bed and leaned against the wall with his shoulder. I swore that I would go back and tell them it was me who found the book and brought it to the room.

'It is OK,' he said finally, 'everything is over now. I already admitted that the book was mine. He has beaten me already.'

All through the night, I could not stop tears from coming from my eyes.

It is midday. Sheikh calls me on the phone and asks me to come to his office immediately. He always says, 'Come when you are done with whatever you are doing.' I wonder what I have done wrong. I try to think if there is anything he asked me to do that I have not done. There is nothing I can think of.

'Salamu alaikum. You sent for me,' I say as I walk into his office.

As I turn and see my aunt's husband, Shuaibu, with his forehead full of wrinkles, I know that something bad has happened.

'Sit,' Sheikh says.

'Allah has caused us a death,' Shuaibu says, avoiding my eyes.

Shuaibu says my Umma suffered much. She stopped eating altogether and threw up anytime they tried to force-feed her. I thought that I would slump over if ever I heard that my mother had died. But hearing now how much she suffered, I feel both sadness and relief in my heart. Relief because Allah has taken away her suffering.

Allah is merciful.

Sheikh wants to come with me and Khadija's husband. But he has to stay for the fundraising. He asks me to leave immediately.

Shuaibu waits outside while I go to the room to get a few things. I put my notebook in my bag first so that I do not forget. As I pack, it does not feel like I am the one stuffing the clothes into the bag. It feels like a film and I am watching myself.

MY WORDS

NAME: Ahmad (Dantala)

PATRON.

1. Regular customer: a customer, especially a regular one, of a shop or business.
2. Sponsor: a giver of money or other support to somebody or something, especially in the arts.
3. Roman slave master: in ancient Rome, somebody who had given a slave his or her freedom but still retained some rights over the former slave.

Sheikh is a <u>PATRON</u> to plenty plenty peoples. He is a patron to Malam Abdul-Nur who is the one keeping all the money for the mosque committee. They have put Malam Abdul-Nur to take care of the six donation boxes around and outside the mosque which ~~have has~~ have FISABILILLAH on the body. It is Adamu and Sheriff that bring the boxes. Adamu and Sheriff are carpenters in the central market. Adamu is Sheikh student and he used to stay at the mosque too until like three years ago when he finish learning

how to be a carpenter from the old carpenter who
died when there was cholera last year. Sheikh is
Adamus patron too. Even as Adamu is not living here
again, Sheikh still have control over him. He (Sheikh)
send Sheriff to be Adamu boy and to live with him
when he run ~~ran~~ away from home and refuse to be
a Shia like his father. That is the first time I am
hearing of a Shia changing to a real Muslim. If you
~~aks~~ ask me, many of the people changing, especially
the ~~Christen~~Christian people who come on Fridays to
be changed when Sheikh is doing his preaching they
come because they think they will get plenty money
when they change to Islam. Sometimes Sheikh find
work for them in office or give them money to start
business, but sometimes they do not get anything. And
when they do not get anything sometimes they go back
to where they came from. Like Isaac who came from
Kaduna and change to be a Muslim and was around
the mosque for like one month thinking maybe he will
get something. He ~~is~~ was complaining about the people
who get things or work or money and one day he just
pack his things and dissappear. Sheikh say some
body saw him in Kaduna where his family is. He has
changed back to being a Christian again. I do not
understand how somebody can change from thinking
that Allah ~~have~~ has a son and then go back and

continue thinking that Allah has a son again. All of the wood things in the mosque and in Sheikhs house is ~~builddone~~ done by Adamu and Sheriff. Sometimes he gives them money like when it is a big job. But when it is small things like donation boxes, they refuse to collect any money from him. Because he is their PATRON.

DESOLATE

1. Empty: bare, uninhabited and deserted.
2. Alone: solitary, joyless and without hope.
3. Grim: dismal and gloomy.

Jibril is DESOLATE these days. The room is desolate too. He (Jibril) comes back when it is night and then he is removing his eyes from my eyes when I look at him. He is talking back to me with MONOSYLLABLES (words consisting of one syllable: a word or sentence consisting of only one syllable, e.g. 'Yes' or 'Me'). Sometimes when he come back I see his face ~~swelling~~ swollen or his eyes red like palm oil or tomato and I have stopped trying to ask why his brother slaps him. I can only guess. I hate guessing. I hate to not be sure of ~~things~~ something.

I am wanting to use DESOLATION in a sentence. I cannot ~~not~~ think how to use it. Jibril will not help me when I ~~oks~~ask him. Just like that the things he knew yesterday he does not know today. He ~~has~~ have even stop speaking English with me and when he see Malam Abdul-Nur coming, he move away from me. It is hard when you have made only one person your friend and that one person is not talking to you. It is not as if you can just meet the other boys that you ~~did~~ do not talk to and just make them your friends. They cannot understand me the way someone like Jibril can understand. And what will I say to those other boys? What will we talk about? They cannot read English, they cannot read Hausa. They do not know words. They laugh at foolish things, they play foolish games like someone messing during prayers or tying a person hands when they ~~have sleep are sleeping~~ have slept. Jibril will not share words with me. I am DESOLATE.

GIBBERISH

1. Nonsense: spoken or written language perceived as unintelligible or devoid of sense.

There are many many things I think are GIBBERISH. Like Christians saying Allah gave a woman ~~pregnant~~pregnancy to give birth to Prophet

Isa (Jesus). Like the hadiths that the Shia people create to show that they are correct. Like all that dancing and singing that some ~~Tarikas darikas~~ Dariqas do that resemble what the Christians do in church.

But what I also think is nonsense is what Malam Abdul-Nur says, that we should stand up and fight against the goverment because they are not doing anything about the Muslims that are killed by those Berom people in Jos and that we should burn all the drinking places and the mosques of those who are not agreeing with us. Especially the burning part. I have done this before and I cannot have that feeling in my body again. He says that those who work for this goverment in any position are working for Shaitan and are making themselves enemies of Islam. I don't know what he means because we all get money and food from Alhaji Usman who is doing contract work with goverment and who is the Governors friend. And Sheikh is in the State Muslim Pilgrims Welfare Board which is also like working for goverment.

The worst for me is that he is calling the people who send their children to university kafiri when he know that Sheikh went to the big university in ~~Egipt~~ Egypt. Sheikh heard him once and told him to stop talking like that and told him that there is

nothing in the Quran or Sunna that says that it is
haram(sin) to work for goverment or to go to university.
Sheikh spoke for long about how Muslims need to get
knowledge anywhere they can find it so that they
can grow stronger in the world and not be defeated
in learning or in science. The only haram is when men
and women are sitting together in the same classes
or stay together in rooms or when boys are allowed
to enter girls rooms. Malam Abdul-Nur agreed and
said sorry. But I have heard him continue saying this
nonsense things when Sheikh is not around, saying that
all the election and voting is kufr and haram and
teaching in university is haram and all working for
government is haram. And some people have started
agreeing with this nonsense.

Even as he is not talking to me, I asked Jibril
what he feel about what Malam Abdul-Nur say. He
opened his mouth to say something but he did not say
anything.

SHRUG

1. Raise and drop shoulders briefly: to raise
   and drop the shoulders briefly, especially to
   indicate indifference or lack of knowledge.

I see the way Jibril is sometimes ~~looking~~ looks when his brother say these things, the way his neck is moving when he swallows spit like someone who is trying not to say something that is in his mind. I see him and I swear there is no INDIFFERENCE (lack of interest in something: lack of interest care or concern) or lack of knowledge in his eyes. He knows what he is thinking but he is fearing to say it, even to me. I can see he does not like it, his eyes do not agree when Malam Abdul-Nur talks about burning, he is grinding his teeth, like me. So when I ask him and he SHRUG, I know that he is lying. I know why he is lying. Me too I will shrug too if Malam Abdul-Nur was my brother. There is something that worry me these days, something I don't have knowledge about. It is how Jibril disappears many nights and doesn't say where he has gone especially when his brother travels.

DISCOVERY

1. Something learned or found: something new that has been learned or found.
2. Process of learning something: the fact or process of finding out about something for the first time.

3. Process of finding something: the process or act of finding something or somebody unexpectedly or after searching.
4. Somebody recognised as potentially successful: a previously unknown musician, actor, performer, or other person who has been identified by somebody as having exceptional talent or unusual beauty.
5. Recognition of potential for success: the recognition of somebody's exceptional talent or beauty, leading to that person's fame.

In all these years, there are many things I did not know that made me open my mouth like how new babies open their mouth. I DISCOVER things these days. Like how Malam Abdul-Nur married quietly last year and have stop ~~tiveing~~ living in the single room in front of Sheikh's house. Like Malam Abdul-Nur has another wife and daughter outside of Ilorin.

I saw Jibril with two small bags of rice, from ~~inside~~ among the rice that Alhaji Usman usually sends to share on Fridays. Even though he still was not talking to me I asked him where he was taking the rice. At first he said it is none of my business. But then his eyes fell down and he started to play with his hands until he started talking and told me everything even the things I didn't ask him. How Malam Abdul-Nurs wife came from one village in Kwara and he did not allowed her to go out or see anybody even other women and she cannot speak Hausa at all at all. How Malam Abdul-Nur was married to another woman before he changed to a Muslim and just disappeared from Ilorin. How the woman stopped talking and became ~~crazy~~mad after she heard that he lived in another town and is ~~was~~ is now a Muslim. How the woman was like a ~~mummy~~ mother to Jibril and paid his school fees.

~~I nearly cried when I heard these new things.~~ And then when I heard about the woman going mad I started telling all the stories inside my head, how my own Umma stop talking and is now more mad each time I go back. How they tie her to the bed until when she need to go to toilet or bathroom or to walk around. They say if she does not walk around her legs will become useless.

Jibril told me he wanted to run away to somewhere far away where his brother will not find him. He said that I should follow him and run away. His brother have two guns under his wife's bed. Jibril said his brother ~~he~~ was talking about burning the Shia people mosque on the other side of town because they abused him in their preaching.

I told him I have nowhere to go. Sheikh is my father. I will not leave my father. I asked him if he will still be a Muslim when he goes. He closed his eyes and then he said yes. He said he likes being a Muslim.

I don't know why I asked, but in my mind I was thinking of how old Jibril was. So I asked him. He said twenty. And I wanted to be the same age with him so I said, I am twenty too. We look like the same age.

I told him that I saw ~~his brother~~ Malam Abdul-Nur remove money from the box at the back of the mosque. I was thinking whether to tell him or not. I thought he will be angry or he will try to say it is a lie. But I saw what I saw. Not once, but twice Malam Abdul-Nur open the donation box and remove money and put in his pockets when he thought no one was looking. Jibril did not look up when I said this. He waited. Then he said that he already knows.

The Land of the Dead

I do not know how to behave towards Shuaibu.

I am grateful that he made the six-hour trip to tell me that my Umma had died. I am grateful that he paid for the white cloth and the gravediggers. While it is hard to forget how he abandoned Khadija because of Umma's sickness, I am sad that because of Umma he had problems with his wife. I want to dislike him. It is easier to dislike him, easier to just tell myself he is a bad man who hated my mother. But I ask myself, What would I have done if I were Shuaibu? What would I have done if the wife that I married no longer had time for me?

In the bus to Dogon Icce I didn't say a word to him. I nodded and shook my head and smiled and shrugged in response to everything he said. And at some point, when he wouldn't stop talking, I pretended to fall asleep. He was talking to me like a man, not like a boy, not like he used to talk to me. He tried to explain everything as if we were members of the same majalisa. When he came to Shiekh's office, he kept putting his hand on my shoulders, as if he had cared for me all my life. I wished, astaghfirullah, that I could push him into a deep well full of soldier ants. But these few hours have calmed my mind and I let it all pass. Allah judges the intentions of the heart.

There is no feeling in my heart or in my head when I meet my brothers Maccido and Hussein. Even with their beards, I recognise them the moment I see them. Hussein's eyes have become more like Umma's; his eyes are deep and have dark circles around them. Their arms are muscular. They look like they have been doing hard exercise.

There are no words between us, only nods and handshakes and salaams. I do not know what to say to these men who have become strangers, who I know nothing about apart from the fact that we used to live in the same home a long, long time ago.

None of us arrived in time for the funeral. The body had started to smell and the men decided to bury her. It is late when we meet and almost time for maghrib prayers.

In the open mosque, we stand shoulder to shoulder, toe to toe, all of us fairly the same height, Maccido only slightly taller than Hussein and I. As we begin to pray, they each drop a small clay tablet in front of them. I am staring at their feet, neat and smooth like those of rich people; there isn't a crack on their heels. The rumours that Shuaibu says he has heard about my brothers are true. They press their foreheads against the tablet as we are praying, refusing to allow their heads to touch the mats; I cannot help staring when I notice that their arms hang down instead of being folded below the chest as we pray. It is all new to me, this Shiite way of praying—like a different religion.

In front of Shuaibu's house, we spread a large mat which is really four mats sewn together. People pass by and pay their condolences. Everyone is so kind in this village. When the last person leaves, we start to talk.

'What of Hassan?' I ask.

'He travelled. He is in Iran.' Hussein says quickly.

Maccido looks at Hussein and shakes his head.

'He died. Last year.'

Suddenly I feel my chest fill up with air and my eyes widen.

'What happened?' I ask.

They both put their heads down.

'What happened?' I ask again.

'We were all in Lebanon for a course. Then Hassan had an accident and died. Please don't tell anyone. We are telling you because you are our brother.'

Maccido is the only one explaining.

'Why? What happened? Why are you not telling me the truth? What kind of course?'

'I am sorry. Please understand. It was a normal Muslim course. We were doing a parade and Hassan had an accident and died.'

'Where was he buried?'

'There. In Lebanon.'

'May Allah forgive him,' I say reluctantly.

For the first time since Shuaibu told me Umma was dead, I feel that pain in the nose that comes before tears. I cry for the brother that I did not know. I look into Hussein's face. The last time I saw them, Hassan and Hussein were identical. I try to imagine how Hassan could have had an accident during a 'course.' They are quiet, refusing to tell me what really happened. I know they are lying. Yes it is Allah's will who lives and who dies but young people do not just die like that without an explanation. My head is spinning as I think of the many things that could have happened, why they were in Lebanon and what made Hussein mention Iran.

Shuaibu has asked Khadija to come live in the house where he and his other wife stay. It is a new house, twice as big as the old one. People say he has been working for some local politician and gets a lot of money.

We roll the mat and take it into the compound. They have put two large mattresses for us in the room adjacent Shuaibu's. I see Khadija briefly as we head in. She has creases on her forehead and grey hair in her eyebrows. There are no smiles left in her eyes, only dullness. She stoops slightly as she walks with a plastic kettle in her hand.

'Sleep well,' she says to us as she makes her way to her room across the open courtyard from ours.

There is silence in the room as we try to arrange the mattresses to sleep. I know it is not his fault but I am angry at my father for sending us to different places. It scares me that I cannot remember his face when I want to be angry with him. I remember him, the things he used to say, his loud voice, but his face is blank in my head. It feels so strange being in the same room as my brothers, who know many things that I don't. They speak to each other in this strange type of Hausa that I barely understand. It sounds like they are singing and dragging the words forcibly from their mouths. I am glad I do not speak this way.

I am angry that my brothers stopped visiting Umma. Maybe if she saw all of her boys she would not have stopped trying to eat, stopped trying to live. Maybe all our faces put together would have been strong enough to break the chains that kept her mouth sealed. What is the use of coming now when they could not visit when she was sick? My head is bursting with questions and I am not sure which to ask first. The anger in my chest is struggling with the questions in my head and stopping them from coming out one by one.

'Are you both still in Tashar Kanuri?' I ask.

'No,' Hussein answers. 'After Tashar Kanuri we went to Zaria, and then to Lebanon and Iran.'

'When our malam in Tashar Kanuri died, people started giving Shiites a hard time there so we decided to move to Zaria, where Shiites are many,' Maccido adds.

He has brought up the issue I have been reluctant to talk about. No one likes Shiites in Sokoto. Everyone believes they are dangerous, especially those of them who go to Iran to study and the Shiite malams who take money from Hezbollah to fight Dariqas and Izalas. Even Sheikh preaches against the way they pray only three times instead of five and how they act so uncivilised during the festival of Ashura, covering themselves with mud and dirt, flogging themselves, even wounding themselves to mourn the killing of Imam Hussein in the battle of Karbala.

'Why do you people observe Ghadir Khum, why do you elevate Ali among the Prophet's companions?' I ask. I really want to know.

'Well, from the hadith of the Prophet, sallallahu alaihi wasallam himself,' Maccido begins. 'I know you yourself have studied under malams, so I am sure you must have heard the hadith: Of whomsoever I am the mawla, Ali is his mawla. O Allah! Love him who loves Ali, hate him who hates Ali.'

'Yes but the Prophet did not praise Imam Ali alone; he had also praised Imam Abu Bakr, Imam Umar and Imam Uthman at different times. There are hadiths that show this. That praise does not make Imam Ali the khalifah. The Prophet did not choose a khalifah to succeed him.'

'Do you really think the Prophet would have left such an important decision to chance? You think the Prophet wanted his people to fight over who would succeed him? Wasn't Imam Ali the only blood relative of the Prophet among the caliphs?'

The way Maccido is speaking with his eyes wide open and Hussein smiling like someone who has just dug up a bag of money, I know I cannot win this argument. It is not that I do not have things to say—about Imam Ali or the fact that they pray only three times a day, combining zuhr and asr in the day time and maghrib and isha at night. I have heard Sheikh debate these things many times and I know the answers and the verses and hadiths to use to counter Shiite teachings. But if you bring up a hadith that clearly says that they are wrong, they will say that the hadith is not authentic. And what can you say when someone says your hadith is fabricated. I am exhausted from arguing and I stop talking. Maccido and Hussein go on and on.

It shouldn't have been like this. I should have been happy to see my brothers, not exhausted or suspicious or confused.

'If you come with us, we can find a place for you, a comfortable place. I know it is hard to understand being a Shiite at first, because everybody spreads lies about us and accuses us of things we do not do, but once you have understood the main things, everything becomes clearer, wallahi.'

I do not respond to Hussein. There is nothing to say to this offer. Maybe I should just respond in kind and ask them to leave their lives, wherever it is that they now are, and come to Sokoto to live under Sheikh. I turn away and begin to roll the prayer beads in my fingers, counting.

The walls are starting to fade and her face is becoming clearer. Someone has broken her chains. She is different from the way she was before she died. Her eyes are not dry or cloudy or lost in their sockets. There is still some flesh on her lanky arms and cheeks. There is that smile deep in her eyes that disappeared with the floods. Her hair is dark and full like it was when Baba, Maccido, Hassan, Hussein and I were all still in Dogon Icce. There is little Hassana on her right and Husseina on her left. I cannot see their faces. Umma does not say any words, but she does not need to: her looks become her thoughts and they move from her eyes into mine. 'Take care of your brothers,' she says. I want to respond. But she puts her slim fingers over my lips. And she smiles. She can hear my thoughts too. She hears that I do not know my brothers anymore. 'They are not bad people,' she adds. 'They are surviving the way they know how, like you.' I nod. A tear rolls down her cheeks. I want to wipe it but my hands will not lift up. She is fading away. I want to scream 'Umma!' but something has caught my throat and mouth and I cannot. Something has pinned me to the bed and it is getting harder and harder to breathe . . .

I wake up to the sound of sweeping in the courtyard and little girls running around and playing. Maccido and Hussein are not in the room. It is daylight already. I cannot remember waking up this late and missing the morning prayer. They should have woken me up.

Shuaibu is sitting on a mat in the courtyard cleaning his teeth with a long chewing stick and spitting out away from the mat.

'Salamu alaikum,' I say.

'Amin, alaikum wassalam,' he replies.

'I am sorry sleep took me away. I realise I missed the morning prayers.'

'Oh, I thought you had left like your brothers. Maccido said they were leaving just as I was performing ablution. I asked him if he would not at least pray with us in the mosque and he said they had prayed already. They just walked out. I couldn't stop them.'

'Where did they say they were going?'

'Are you asking me? They left the way they came, like spirits. Like a breeze they vanished. This is what being Shiite has taught them. To disregard people. Those boys are up to no good, wallahi. I see it in their eyes. Those were not the eyes of normal people. I can swear it. If it wasn't for our family relationship, would I have let ungrateful Shiites enjoy my home and hospitality? You just be glad they didn't get you mixed up in whatever nonsense they are mixed up in. I don't know how someone can be raised in the right way and decide to go and become a Shiite.'

Sometimes you do a thing and you wish you could step out of your body and slap yourself, give yourself a good beating. That is how I feel for not waking up. I walk back into the room and find that Khadija has kept hot koko and kosai for me. I lift my bag to take out my phone and I discover a rolled-up bundle of money bound with a yellow rubber band beneath it. I open the roll and a white piece of paper with a number on it falls out. I count the money. Twenty thousand naira. That's how much my brothers left me. I fold the white paper and put it in my pocket and drop the money in my bag.

Jibril is on my mind. They must be working like donkeys now because today is the fund-raising event. He has sent me a text in English saying just, 'How are you?' This is the first time he has sent me a text message and it feels strange reading from him in English, even though we speak a lot of English. Seeing the words on the screen of my phone makes it different. I reply.

'I am fine. They have buried her. How is the fund-raising?'

'Fine. Plenty work. We will finish today,' he texts back.

I like speaking in English to Jibril, especially when I do not want the other boys to know what I am saying to him. I miss it. I wish I'd brought something in English to read; it didn't cross my mind because we left in such a hurry.

Shuaibu is out and Khadija sits on her own mat on the right side of the courtyard. She calls out my name.

'Come and sit with an old woman and tell her stories,' she says.

I am a bit uncomfortable. I do not want her to say things about Umma that will make my nose hurt.

'Do you know I did not cry?' she begins. 'What crying will I cry, when tears have been taken away from me a long time ago? Ah, if they had told me that a person exhausts her tears I would have sworn that it wasn't true. I cried for my husband. I cried for Umma. I cried for my empty womb. Every day. So when Umma died, I looked for tears. I hit my chest and shook my stomach, but nothing. The tears of an old woman were finished.'

I start to fiddle. I cannot look in her eyes.

'Is everything well where you are? Tell me. Don't say fine, tell me how it really is.'

'Honestly, I am thankful. Our malam is very kind and has a good heart. The room that they gave me I share with only one person, the younger brother of Sheikh's deputy. I don't have a problem of food or anything.'

'Have you learned any trade?'

'No.'

'Why?'

I have never thought of learning a trade before. Maybe because Sheikh has given me everything I need and hasn't asked me to work on his farm like the rest of the boys.

'You know that if anything happens to that malam of yours, kind as he is, when his property is being shared among his family, you will not even be called. You will be out on the street in a minute. The sooner you start learning a trade, the better for you. You cannot remain a boy to a malam forever. You will marry and have your own family. What will you feed them? Or is it your malam who will feed your wife and children?'

I nod. For the first time I think of what I would do without Sheikh.

Dogon Icce has changed over the last few months. There are now two boreholes, one dug by the local government chairman situated near the village head's house and another which Khadija says was paid for by the politician Shuaibu is working for. He was a former member of the Sokoto State House of Assembly who now wants to contest for the House of Representatives.

Everything is greener now because of the rains. The footpaths have been eaten by the grass and there are little puddles everywhere. Lizards run across footpaths and on walls, all looking very busy. Sometimes I wonder if these animals look at us too and wonder what we are doing moving around. Gobedanisa used to like killing lizards and opening their stomachs to see what was in them. Sometimes he would find one that had tiny eggs in it. Gobedanisa and Acishuru used to place bets with their wee-wee about who would first kill a lizard with eggs in it. I too started killing lizards with them. I think I might be going crazy but it seems like every lizard is looking at me. Maybe they can feel that I once played games with their lives. I asked Sheikh about this and he told me this hadith: 'There is no man who kills even a sparrow or anything smaller without its deserving it, but Allah will question him about it.' He asked me to read about it. I like that Sheikh always asks me to go and read more about anything I ask. From his library he brought out a small book which had a chapter called 'Animals in Islam' and said if I could read English he would have given it to me. That was the day he found out I could read English. I told him I had been learning it with Jibril. He was so happy. 'You will go far, insha Allah,' he said. Then he said that his library was mine and gave me the book. In it I read another hadith which I cannot forget, and that makes me now scared of killing anything I will not eat: 'He who takes pity even on a sparrow and spares its life, Allah will be merciful on him in the day of judgement.' But sometimes, Allah forgive me, I miss killing lizards.

I am thinking of an English book in Sheikh's library that I really want to read called *Baba of Karo*, which is still wrapped in transparent polythene. I don't know if Sheikh will let me tear it open or if perhaps he wants to give it to someone else. The back of the book says that it is a life story of an old Hausa woman and it stretches from the late nineteenth century until the first half of the twentieth.

I asked Jibril about centuries and why it is that the nineteenth century is made up of all the eighteen hundred years while the twentieth is made up of all the nineteen hundred years. This is confusing. The way Jibril kept stuttering while he was explaining it made me sure that he too didn't really know.

Since Sheikh found out I know how to read English, everything has become different. He gives me the key to his office when he is going out. There are things he tells me—his plans for the future—that scare me. Big plans that I am not supposed to tell anyone. The school is only the beginning of what he wants. 'As far as Niger and Mali' is how far he wants to take this movement. The movement will organise our operations but Sheikh is also tired of people referring to him as a 'dan Izala. Yes he studied once under the founder of the Izala movement, but 'I am not an Izala,' he says. He wants the movement to set him apart.

It is good to be away from all the noise around the motor park in Sokoto. Here I can hear my heart beat and when a metal bucket drops on the floor at night the sound bursts into the silence like something exploding. Silence is good, but sometimes noise is also good.

The sugarcane here is sold in long, fat pieces. The way the skin is scraped you would think they had competitions for who could scrape the cleanest. Few things are like sugarcane. When I want to chew it, I do not like having one or two small sticks because that will just make me want more and if I cannot have it, then I will be irritated that the longing for it has been created in me. But these long fat ones, they make you remember Allah's goodness. I wonder sometimes if aljanna will have sugar cane. In Bayan Layi, I asked Malam Junaidu about this and he said that, insha Allah, aljanna will have sweeter things. I still wonder what things can be sweeter than this sugar cane. Perhaps it is just santi talking—santi is an enjoyment of food that makes you close your eyes and say and do foolish things—but I think that maybe we should know if aljanna will have sugar cane.

I am belching and chewing and swallowing. I reach the very last bit and it falls from my hand. As I struggle to save it from reaching the dusty floor I step on it. I want to scream. I am annoyed. There is something about the last piece of anything. It is like the enjoyment is summarised in that last piece—it is the final thing that makes the experience complete. Except if you deliberately throw it or give it away, losing that last piece is like going on a long journey to deliver a message, then finding upon arriving that you left it at home. I pick up and examine the piece of sugar cane that I have stepped on. It cannot be saved. Reluctantly I throw it back to the ground. All the santi is gone with that last piece.

I am sitting with Shuaibu and two other men on the large mat in front of his house just after maghrib. The older man with a full white beard starts talking about Alhaji Usman. At first I do not realise it is the same Alhaji Usman I know, until they start talking about the things he has, like his brother's fish farm in Kebbi, which is really his.

'I hear he is contesting for Senate,' Shuaibu says.

'I thought it was governor,' the man with the white beard says. The other man has fallen asleep.

'No, it is Senate. I hear he has been speaking to people.'

'Is he not the one whose first son left the house to join the big Shiite malam in Sokoto?'

'Yes, him. Ah, he has since disowned that son. His other son works in England. That one doesn't want to come back.'

'Allah forbid,' the sleeping man mutters. 'I would rather an aggressive Izala who takes everything literally than a Shiite who creates a different religion out of Islam.' He makes chewing movements and dozes off again.

'I don't blame his son for not wanting to come back, everything is tough here,' the old man says.

'But everything is tough everywhere,' Shuaibu responds, 'don't you listen to BBC Hausa? They too complain.'

'Hmmm. I hear the man builds mosques all over Sokoto.'

'Or is he doing it to buy votes?'

'How does that concern me? Allah knows what is in his heart. All I can see is that he is building mosques and helping people.'

'Your talk is true.'

I do not know if Sheikh knows. From being with him all these years I know that he doesn't like to openly support any candidate. During the last elections he gathered all the people who come to his mosque and gave a speech at the primary school football field. Even though he said that everyone should go out, register and vote and let their wives also go out and vote, he did not say anything about which candidate to vote for.

'Let your women study,' Sheikh said, 'and let them vote. Let them learn how to read. The wives of Christians read and write and our wives cannot even read the Quran. There is no sin if a man accompanies his wives to go and queue up to register or to vote.'

Some men didn't like what he said at first. But after he explained the importance of numbers in elections, most people were convinced about letting their wives go out to register and to vote. All of us who follow Sheikh voted for the same party. But he told us he would not force anyone to do anything. I wonder what he will do during the next elections, especially if Alhaji Usman is really contesting.

My phone rings as we are praying isha. Shuaibu looks angrily at me and turns away. Thankfully the prayer is just about to end. It is Jibril. I call him back but he does not respond. Then he sends a text.

'Sheikh's car was attacked! They shot him!'

I keep trying his number but he is not picking up. I cannot breathe.

'Is Sheikh OK?' I text back.

'I don't know. But Umar and Sambo are dead.'

Umar and Sambo are the two big men who have been guarding Sheikh when he goes out or when he travels. I keep trying to call Jibril until the phone says that his number is switched off.

I throw two oranges from the tray of food into my packed bag for when I get hungry on my way back home. I put the little knife in the side pocket of the bag. Peeling oranges with my fingers has always been difficult for me. I always make a mess of it.

I cannot eat or sleep or stop my hands from shaking. As soon as the sun rises I will leave this place. Shuaibu will say that I am acting all crazy because I'm more upset that they have shot my malam than I was when my own mother died. I don't care. I just need to get out of this village as soon as possible.

TERRIFY

1. Make somebody very frightened: to make somebody feel very frightened or alarmed.
2. Intimidate somebody: to coerce somebody to do something by using threats.

Women TERRIFY me. Even though Sheikh have take the book I still think of the Every Woman book. Since I read this book, all women make me ~~fear~~ afraid. All the things that happen in their bodies like MENSTRUATION (I can never pronounce that word) make me feel like when they are walking around their bodies are always doing something or growing something or making something. I think that women are strong to be walking around and doing their work with all those things happening to them. Women should not work.

Many things TERRIFY me. How easy it is for Malam Abdul-Nur to say the word kill especially when he is talking about the Shia people and the Dariqas.

When Sheikh travel and Malam Abdul-Nur is the one preaching, he say plenty bad bad things about them. I believe that the Shia people and Dariqas are wrong in the way they are doing their Islam. But I ~~did~~ do not agree with the way Malam Abdul-Nur is talking about them like he will kill all of them if he catch them. He says that the Shia people are more bad than the Christians. I don't understand how a Muslim can be more bad than Christians who believe that Allah ~~have~~has a child. He says that the Dariqa people worship human ~~beem~~being and put the picture of their leader Inyass all over their house and car and ~~machine~~ motorcycle as if Inyass is Prophet Mohammed. Everyone is ~~fearing~~ afraid of Malam Abdul-Nur and of how he is shaking when he is talking. But it is easy to forget where you are when he is talking because his preaching is very sweet and he knows all the Sunna and Quran. I think he likes to TERRIFY people.

In the night yesterday some people put X in red paint all over the mosque wall. Sheikh say that maybe it is just some bad boys in the area but Malam Abdul-Nur say it was the Shia people. He say that since Sheriff leave the Shia people and come and join us they had been saying things, bad bad things about us. Sheikh asked him (Malam

Abdul-Nur)where he heard this and Malam Abdul-
Nur kept talking about how bad they are and how
they are making trouble in other countries. Then he
start saying we need to protect ourselves. Always he
will be saying we need to protect ourselves. I do not
know what the meaning of that is.

   Before Sheikh take the book I ~~am~~ was talking
with some boys in the motor park who all agree that
letting a girl rub your penis until sperm come out can
make the girl pregnant. They said the sperm enter
women through their skin. I tried to explain to them
what I read about women in the book. But I don't know
what CONCEPTION is in Hausa and when I said it in
English they all start ~~taughting~~ laughing and saying I
was trying to deceive them by talking nonsense they
cannot understand. I wanted to show them the book,
but then I did not want everyone to know that the
book is in our room. So I left them alone and let them
keep thinking I was saying rubbish. And now Sheikh
have take the book. They are hopeless those boys.

Blood for Blood

I am lying down with my bag in the open area of the hospital. I am exhausted from waiting and from travelling. Jibril has gone home to do some work for his brother. The two men from the mosque guarding Sheikh's room are not allowing anyone through except his family, Malam Abdul-Nur and the hospital staff. I am not going anywhere until I see Sheikh.

As I step outside to pee by the bushes, I see a crowd of Sheikh's followers gathering in front of the hospital and many police cars driving in. The police are pushing people back and keeping them away from the hospital gate. I walk past the ward where they say the oldest patient in the hospital is. Everyone says he has been here for many years. Sometimes he goes unconscious for months and just when they think he might not make it, he wakes up. Only Allah knows what type of sickness that is that makes a man go to sleep for months.

I stand in front of a large tree behind the hospital wards and start to pee. I don't want to squat because the grass is thick everywhere around. Suddenly a tall, fair girl in a light green hijab appears from behind the bushes. I struggle to turn away but I am right in the middle of peeing and cannot stop it. My caftan drops from under my chin and I pee all over myself. The girl is embarrassed too and turns away. As she walks past in the direction of the shops that sell provisions, she covers her face and giggles. I go to the tap to try and rinse off the urine.

'I am afraid,' Jibril texts.

'Me too,' I reply.

I want to ask him why he is afraid so I can tell him why I am afraid. I am afraid that if Sheikh dies, Malam Abdul-Nur will change towards me. Alhaji Usman may stop sending us money and the new movement will die before it has even started. I do not know where I will go or what I will do. I can't even get in to see Sheikh and no one will tell me anything about how he is. It feels like Khadija's words are already coming true.

I see the girl who just laughed at me pass by in the hallway of the wards. She is carrying two large bottles of water. She has a mole on the right side of her face and has a pointed nose like I see in the pictures of Indian actresses. Her eyes—it is her eyes that make me freeze. They are bright and look like a deep gully, the type that pulls you and makes you dizzy when you look down into it. Everything has slowed down—it is taking forever for her to walk past. She walks right through the men guarding Sheikh's ward and into the room.

I lie down on one of the benches and use my bag as a pillow. The crowd outside is getting more and more agitated and there are sirens blaring all over the place. Images of my last day in Bayan Layi keep flashing in my mind. It is getting harder and harder to block it out. These days the face of the Big Party man that I struck stays in my head. I wonder about his wives and children. I wonder if they still remember him or if like my father's face, his face is fading from their heads.

There are two gunshots in quick succession. People in the crowd are screaming. I run to the part of the wall that has hollow bricks and peep. I see one policeman waving his gun in the air. The nurses are asking people to stay down. People begin to scamper to safety away from the shots. A hospital attendant drags me by my clothes and asks me to stay down. More shots are fired and by the fifth shot we are all on the ground, some praying, some screaming, some crying.

'Police are shooting here,' I text Jibril.

I keep looking at my phone for the message that says my text has been delivered. I try to call him. His phone is switched off. It is annoying when I call someone and their phone is switched off.

The police start to disperse the crowd. Slowly people get up, dusting their clothes and sighing. Some are laughing embarrassedly because of how they screamed like babies during the shooting. I walk back to my bench.

The girl in the green hijab comes out of the ward with a stainless steel plate in her hands. I feel like the bench is about to collapse as she walks directly towards me. She hands me the plate, which has rice and beans with stew and fish. For a moment I hesitate, then stretch out my hands to take the food.

'Let me find a cup to get you water,' she says.

'Are you here for Sheikh?' I ask.

'You don't know me?' she asks, 'Are you not the one who stays at the mosque?'

I can't remember seeing her. I know that Sheikh has four daughters, two of whom are married, but I have never seen any one of them.

'How is he?' I ask.

'He just woke up. They got him in the chest and right arm.'

'Is he talking?'

'Not yet. They have gone to get blood. They say he lost a lot of blood but, insha Allah, nothing will happen to him.'

She turns and walks away. I want to ask her name but I feel like this is the wrong time. She has fire in her blood, this one. There is no pity or worry in her voice. She looked defiant the way she bunched her lips and lifted her finger when she said: 'Insha Allah, nothing will happen to him.'

Alhaji Usman comes into the hospital ward with two armed policemen behind him. He is wearing only a caftan instead of his usual babban riga and he looks very grave with his hands behind his back. I get up to greet him but he doesn't seem to recognise me. The two men guarding the ward give way to let them through.

Jibril calls me back. He is whispering and panting. I cannot make out anything he is saying and then the line goes dead. His phone is switched off when I call him back. Now I am really scared and I call Malam Abdul-Nur's number. His number too is switched off. I take my bag and leave the hospital.

On the road leading away from the hospital, there are dozens of policemen. Black smoke rises from burning tyres. They are not letting any motorcycles pass in front of the hospital, and cars are stopped and searched. I walk quickly, hoping to turn off this street and find a motorcycle or a Keke Napep.

Then a skinny policeman shouts, asking me to stop, aiming his gun at my chest. I stop.

'What are you carrying?' he screams.

'Nothing,' I reply.

'Open it!' he orders.

I zip open the bag.

'Turn it upside down!'

I hesitate. He cocks his gun and I turn the bag upside down. A few clothes fall to the ground.

'Everything!'

I shake until the bag is almost empty.

'Throw it on the ground and put your hands behind your head!'

I obey and he kicks the bag around while still pointing his gun at my chest. The little knife I took from Shuaibu's house rolls out as well as my money wrapped in a paper. He looks at the knife, looks at me, then reaches forward and kicks my knee so that I fall to the ground. He kicks me in the stomach so hard I throw up all the rice and beans and fish I have just eaten.

'Get up,' he says. 'You want to stab me with a knife ko?'

'It is for oranges!'

He slaps me and asks me to run. I leave everything behind, running and stumbling. Two other policemen laugh as I do.

On many walls there is the inscription Haqiqi in either char-coal or red paint. In front of the mosque I see a new huge white sign with 'Jama'atul Ihyau Islamil Haqiqiy' written in bold blue letters. The logo is a crescent and a star. The low fence is being built up and there are concrete blocks, cement

bags, tiles, heaps of sand and rocks in front of the mosque.
Inside our room the new paint still smells fresh and there
are two new beds and mattresses. This is not the room I left
a few days ago.

Jibril is not here and his number is still switched off. I
am fidgeting. Even the motor park is quiet. Malam Abdul-
Nur's office is locked. I ask the other boys in the mosque if
any of them has seen Jibril. I hear the boys laughing behind
me when I turn away. I never pay them heed. If I wasn't so
desperately looking for Jibril I would not even speak to them.

As darkness falls, people gather in front of the mosque.
Mostly people I do not remember seeing. Malam Abdul-Nur
arrives in one of Sheikh's buses with two huge bearded men
on either side of him and Jibril following closely behind. My
eyes meet Jibril's and he looks away.

Malam Abdul-Nur leads the prayer. I have never seen so
many people in the mosque in my life. The mosque is fuller
than the huge Juma'at mosque on Fridays. There are people
standing outside on either side of the mosque. My stomach
hurts from the policeman's kick—I do not know if it is this or
the sheer number of bodies in the mosque that is making it
difficult to breathe. The two huge bearded men are standing
guard and not praying with the rest of us. They are scanning
the crowd, angrily, grinding their teeth as if to scare anyone
planning on attacking Malam Abdul-Nur.

No one moves after the prayer. One of the bodyguards
brings Malam Abdul-Nur a chair while Jibril sets up the microphone. It is as if everyone knows something I don't.

Malam Abdul-Nur starts to speak, first slowly, but increas-
ingly the veins of his neck begin to bulge like fat millipedes

under his skin. He starts with a sermon about shirk, about how people worship other persons apart from Allah.

'There is nothing worse than shirk, and in this matter some Christians are better than the Shiites. You know there are some Christians who don't elevate Prophet Jesus to the position of Allah and they believe that there is no one worthy of worship but Allah. They just don't call Him Allah. Surely then, the Shiites, who set up gods in opposition to Allah, are worse than Christians. Allah says in the last verse of Surah Al-Fath: Mohammed is the messenger of Allah and those with him are severe against the disbelievers and merciful among themselves.'

All around there is silence and you can even hear people breathing. The only thing that breaks the silence is the thunderous sound of 'Allahu Akbar' that follows. There are goose pimples all over my skin. Malam Abdul-Nur is in total control of the crowd. He starts to cry when he talks of our brothers who were shot. He is wagging his finger and he is crying.

'What have we ever done to the Shiites? What have we ever done but be merciful to them? We do not even follow the command of Allah to be severe against them. How do they repay our mercy? By killing our brothers. By shooting our Sheikh on the very day we launch our movement. But they cannot stop us. They cannot stop Jama'atul Ihyau Islamil Haqiqiy!'

The crowd roars and begins chanting, 'Haqiqiy! Haqiqiy!' The fat man sitting to my right is chanting and crying and wiping his tears with his stubby fingers.

I wish I wasn't sitting right in the centre of the mosque, where everyone will see me if I get up. The hot tears that are flowing from my eyes down my cheeks—I do not know where they are from. But I know they are not from the sermon. I am trapped—in this mosque full of anger and tears, in my body full of pain, in my head full of confusion, in my heart full of fear. I do not know anything. I do not know what is happening to Sheikh or what Jibril is thinking.

As the crowd begins to disperse I sneak away to the hospital.

There are two policemen where the bodyguards were standing earlier in the day. I lie down on the bench opposite the one I sat on before, which is now occupied by two older women. I turn, facing the wall, still wincing in pain from the kick, and start to see my mother again.

Sometimes I wish I knew why Allah does his things. Why He lets good people get shot and bad people get all the glory; why He lets bad people have such gifts like the power to move crowds and convince people and make grown men cry. It is His earth.

Early in the morning I walk around the hospital to look for a mosque. There is one not far from the gate. By the time I finish my ablution, the prayer has just begun. I quickly join the row of six men behind the man leading the prayer.

I wander around a bit afterward before I go to where the shops are to see if any one of them is open. In the first open one I see, a man is scooping sugar into little transparent polythene bags. I think he was one of the men I prayed with at the mosque earlier. His eyes are lined with tozali. I will check the dictionary in Sheikh's office when I go back for the English word for tozali. As our eyes meet he rests his left wrist on his waist like a woman. He reminds me of the 'dan daudu who shouted at me when I went to watch dambe a long time ago. Maybe he is a 'dan daudu too.

'What do you want?' he asks and calls me samari, young person. I hate being called samari. I hate the way he sings his words with an annoying lisp.

'Batteries, the small ones.'

'How many?'

'Four.'

I turn around and see the girl from yesterday standing behind me.

'Good morning,' she says.

'Good morning,' I reply.

'Yesterday you just left my plate and cup and went away.'

'In the name of Allah forgive me. I didn't see you when I was leaving.'

'No problem. It is OK.'

'How is Sheikh?' I ask paying for the batteries.

'He woke up last night. He is stronger now, Alhamdulillah.'

'Alhamdulillah!'

She asks for two big bottles of water.

'I wish I could see him,' I say.

'Why can't you see him? I know he will be glad to see you.'

'The men won't let me in.'

I pay for her water. 'Thank you,' she says and adds, 'follow me. Don't say anything. Just follow me.'

I walk behind her into the ward, inserting the batteries into my small radio. She turns around and asks me to hold the bottles of water. I don't know why I didn't think of it. I feel embarrassed.

'He is our relative,' she says to the policemen, who look at me suspiciously.

She doesn't wait for them to say anything. 'Come,' she says and walks past them. I look down as I walk between the two officers.

There are two women in the room. One of them I know is his wife. She is making pap beside the bed. Sheikh looks strange without anything covering his head. His right arm is wrapped in bandages, as is the right part of his chest. He stretches his left arm and I take it with both my hands, slowly, afraid to hurt him.

'Where have you been?' he says, smiling.

'I have been outside, ya Sheikh. Since yesterday. I came as soon as I could. It was Jibril who sent me a message.'

'What were you doing outside?'

'They wouldn't let me in.'

'You could've just told them you are my boy. Anyway, how are things? I heard there was some disturbance here yesterday.'

'Yes ya Sheikh. But everything is OK now.'

'I hope people aren't too angry. I have told Abdul-Nur to give them my message. We must not lose our heads over this. You know what happened in Iraq? The enemies of Islam and of the people, after the Americans turned the country upside down, what did they do? They went to Sunni mosques and bombed Sunni mosques. They went to Shiite mosques and bombed Shiite mosques. And then people started attacking each other. Very easily they started civil war. Who gains and who loses? I have seen too much of this kind of thing. I know it. This will pass. We will not give them power by getting angry. I told Abdul-Nur no one must talk about this. We have buried our dead. Allah is greater than they are.'

I feel the pain in my nose. It would be a disgrace to cry here in front of these women. The girl in the green hijab takes the bowl of pap and a little plate of kosai and puts it on a tray that hangs from the metal railings of the bed. He spills some pap on his chest as he tries to eat with his trembling left hand. She cleans him up and tries to take the spoon from him.

'Aisha, please let me try,' he says with a smile. He sits up and breathes heavily. After the third spoonful he turns to me.

'How was the funeral?'

'It was OK. They had finished before we got there.'

'Allah forgive her. May Allah give her rest.'

He turns to the women in the room and tells them that my mother just died.

'Allah Sarki! May Allah grant her repose,' Sheikh's wife says.

'May Allah grant her repose,' Aisha repeats after the second woman.

'You will do something for me,' Sheikh says. 'Remind me please before you go.'

Aisha gets up from the chair and leans against Sheikh's bed. I shake my head and tell her she should sit. After going back and forth about it, I accept and sit down. Alhaji Usman opens the door, panting. He stares at Sheikh.

'Please give us a few minutes,' Sheikh says to his wife. 'Not you,' he adds when I get up too.

'This one is my son,' he says to Alhaji Usman.

'They have burnt down the big Shiite mosque on Balewa Way,' Alhaji Usman says. His eyes are red and he is raising his cap and running his hands through his hair repeatedly.

'Do you know who did it?'

'Who else? That one that you won't let go. He will be your ruin, wallahi, Sheikh.'

'I gave him specific instructions not to even raise the issue.'

'I don't even know if anyone died. But they torched everything, including the malam's house behind the mosque.'

'Do me this one favour, Alhaji. He is stubborn as a donkey, but not useless. I still need him. A time will come to throw him away. But that time is not now.'

'What do you want Sheikh?'

'I will send him away to do some work for me.'

'Where?'

'Saudi Arabia.'

'Even for me that is hard. And they will soon start looking for him. I don't want anyone to associate him with me.'

'There is a way. He will go across by road to Kano and to Maradi, where he will lay low with an old student of mine. Then he will go to Niamey and travel to Saudi Arabia from there.'

'OK. But Sheikh, I will not be involved in any more of this kind of rubbish. One more thing and I will have to insist that he goes.'

'Please trust me on this. Just let's get him out today. Two, three months. He will calm down.'

'What is your name?' Alhaji Usman asks me.

'Ahmad,' I tell him.

'Arabic and Quran, he knows very well, one of my best assets. He is even trying with English,' Sheikh adds.

'Can he come work for us on the campaign?'

'Ah no, not this one. I need him, especially now that Abdul-Nur will be gone. I am getting old, I need someone smart to stand with me.'

'What do we do about the attack? I don't want retaliation and more retaliation.'

'I know the malam. We disagree and do debates but he is a reasonable man. Let us call him. We will offer to rebuild their mosque.'

'But you know what people will say if they know we are building a Shiite mosque.'

'Yes, allow me to handle that. I will talk to him. We were at Barewa College together, I went to Cairo and he went to Iran.'

Alhaji Usman shakes Sheikh's left hand, drops a black polythene bag on the bed and walks out.

'Open the bag,' Sheikh tells me.

'Count it. Not everything, just the bundles.'

I have never seen so many crisp notes in my life before. There are ten bundles of one thousand naira notes. He opens the small black purse by his side and pulls out two five hundred naira notes.

'Take this for transport. You will go with the driver and one of those policemen to the bank. Unity Bank, the one just opposite the Juma'at mosque. Aisha will give you the account details.'

I protest telling him that I will not need the transport money since the driver is taking me. He ignores my protest and asks me to go. I am dizzy just thinking that I am holding one million naira in my hands.

Outside the ward, on the bench, Aisha writes down the account details on a sheet of paper. My hands tremble a bit as I receive it by the tip, careful not to touch her hand. She looks up at me and smiles showing one dimple on her right cheek. I cannot look into her eyes. I walk away quickly, the policeman following closely behind.

SHEET

I am happy that I know the difference of piece of
paper and sheet of paper. It use to worry me. But now
I know piece of paper is paper that is not complete
that somebody tear to write something and sheet of
paper is a full paper that is complete.

KOHL

The English word for TOZALI is KOHL. Jibril ~~say~~ said
he has never heard the word before. Sheikh said he
has never heard the word before. Nobody has heard
the word KOHL before.

Brotherly Love

It is hard to understand how it is that big men feel safe with all the policemen around them. Since we started having all these roadblocks and these policemen, who search cars and make people push their motorcycles all along the road in front of our mosque, I have felt afraid.

I feel more unsafe now than the day our mosque was attacked, the week that Malam Abdul-Nur left for Maradi. I did not sleep that night. People threw firebombs over the fence starting a fire that gutted Sheikh's office and half of the mosque. I had my key to the office and everyone thought I was crazy when, instead of running out, I opened Sheikh's office to try and get some books out. But the heat and the smoke overwhelmed me. In all of the things that have been happening, it is this that made me angry—all those books from Egypt and Saudi Arabia and London, all gone. It would have been preferable if my room and all the other rooms got burnt but not Sheikh's office, which was packed top to bottom with books. That was the day my anger towards the Shiites began. But my fear, it began with those police uniforms, those guns, those roadblocks. My fear was fed each time by the petrified faces of motorcyclists, afraid of being made to do frog jumps for offences as little as looking too directly into a policeman's eyes. Or being made to roll in the dust while being slapped and kicked.

The day of the attack, Sheikh made one of the drivers take him from the hospital with all his bandages to the field where people had gathered, angry, ready to burn down every Shiite mosque and house. He winced as he screamed. He said he would rather die than have them start a war with the Shiites. At first they wouldn't listen, but he screamed until he found the words that made them calm, that made them pay attention.

Tomorrow is the big meeting. Sheikh made me get a new white caftan sewn even though I insisted that the one I was planning to wear was still fairly new. I am going with Sheikh to take notes, together with Malam Yunusa, Malam Abduljalal and Malam Hamza, who are all also trustees of Jama'atul Ihyau Islamil Haqiqiy. I am surprised Malam Hamza will be there. The last I heard of him, he was very ill at home. The deputy governor is the chairman of the reconciliation committee set up by the governor to settle the issues between the Shiites and us. All the other men proposed by the governor were rejected either by the Shiites or by Sheikh. The Shiites rejected the head of the Muslim Pilgrims Board because Sheikh was also on that board. Sheikh rejected Alhaji Usman, even though the Shiites themselves wanted him, because he didn't want anyone to say that Alhaji Usman was our patron and accuse him of taking sides at the end. And, when someone suggested that it would be wrong to hold any reconciliation meeting without the Sultan of Sokoto, everyone agreed that he should be an observer on the committee.

I have not been able to sleep since Sheikh told me that I will follow him to the deputy governor's office. The temptation to tell Jibril everything that Sheikh wants me to do with him is very strong but I keep quiet because I don't want it to sound like I am bragging. Especially now that I have started singing the call to prayer at the mosque. Wallahi, I love it more than I ever thought I would. Closing my eyes, covering one ear with my hand, holding the microphone with the other and singing:

Allahu Akbar
Allahu Akbar
Allahu Akbar
Allahu Akbar
Ash hadu anla ila ha illallah
Ash hadu anla ila ha illallah
Ash hadu anna Muhammadan Rasulullah
Ash hadu anna Muhammadan Rasulullah
Hayya alas salah
Hayya alas salah
Hayya alal falah
Hayya alal falah . . .

It transports me to a deep place away from everything around me. The feeling is one of being lost inside myself, a dark, peaceful place. My lungs empty as I drag out each line: I breathe in to refill my lungs and empty them again. I am lost in that dark space until I say the last words 'La ilaha illallah.' I try to explain to Jibril but he cannot understand how just singing these words can give me the best feeling in the world, a feeling that drives out all pain, all fear, all worry, all want. I made him try it in the room; I told him to cover his ear, breathe in, relax and pretend that no one was there, not even himself. He still didn't get the feeling. You can tell when a muezzin is enjoying the call or when he is doing it just because he has to, like Abu, who yawns into the microphone when he has to call the fajr prayers. If it was up to me, Abu would never call a prayer.

I spread out the white caftan on the bed and dust the black shoes that Suraj the shoeshiner polished last night. The plastic folder has plain sheets of paper, a notebook, a red pen and a blue pen. It will be a real disaster if I doze off during the meeting especially as I am there to take notes. My eyes are heavy from a night spent staring at the ceiling instead of sleeping.

Alhaji Usman has sent two of his new jeeps for Sheikh to ride in: one with tinted glass and one without. Sheikh resisted very strongly, saying he didn't want to go in a borrowed car. But Alhaji Usman told him that it was better to use the jeep just so we wouldn't have a hard time getting into Government House. The thought crossed my mind, that if Sheikh collects money from Alhaji Usman, using his cars for just one day shouldn't be a problem.

Sheikh is still at home. He went back home after the morning prayers to take a nap. Since he got shot, he has been sleeping much more. He cannot speak for as long as he used to. Last Friday, his tafsir was quite short and he was panting the whole time. Perhaps I just hadn't noticed but his beard seems to have grown greyer in the three weeks since he returned from hospital. I worry when I walk into his office and find him lost in thought. Sometimes he flinches or ducks as if something was flying in to hit him. The first few times I ducked too, until I realised it was all in his head.

When Sheikh arrives, we split into two groups. Sheikh, Malam Yunusa and I enter the jeep with tinted glass while Malam Abduljalal and Malam Hamza enter the second one. Behind and in front of us are buses containing some of the men who guard Sheikh when he goes out. The deputy governor has also sent a police car to escort us.

The car seats are new and cold. The air smells fresh, like the type of nice expensive chewing gum that Malam Abdul-Nur sometimes chews—the type they sell sometimes in go-slows, only better. It smells exactly like how I imagine it to be in London or Dubai or Cairo or Saudi Arabia. A screen on the dashboard shows what is behind the car when the driver tries to reverse. The dashboard is so clean I have a strong urge to touch it, just rub my hands over it. I do not know when the car is on or when it is off because the engine makes barely any noise and I feel no vibration at all. Kai! The cold is making me want to pee.

No one stops us on the way because of the police car. In the mirror, I see Sheikh sweating. He is breathing hard and leaning away from the door. I turn around and see him counting the beads on his wooden chasbi. He does not look well.

We are the first to arrive. I use the opportunity to ask where the toilets are. The tiles inside are not like the tiles in our mosque. Everything is so white and shiny and I feel like I will slip and fall. I am afraid to mess up the toilet seat so I squat over the seat and aim carefully. I could eat in this place.

The big Shiite malam comes with three men. Everyone shakes hands and does introductions. Sheikh refers to me as Malam Ahmad. No one has referred to me like this before and it makes me feel important. I am glad when the deputy governor walks in with the Sultan, because the silence in the room was very awkward and everyone was trying not to look at each other. I think for a moment about my brothers. One day, they will be Shiite malams too.

The deputy governor has so many people around him. He has someone holding his bag, someone pulling out a chair for him, someone holding his phones and someone writing when he speaks. I wonder why one man needs so many people as if he were a cripple. Sheikh does not even let me carry his bag.

It is hard to take notes when no one will speak straight. Everyone except Sheikh and the big Shiite malam speaks in circles and says many unnecessary things before getting to the point. I hope that the paper I have will be enough.

The men with the Shiite malam are all speaking so angrily. I am afraid that this meeting might end in a fight. I am afraid that Sheikh might get angry and the whole meeting will just be a waste of time.

'I assume I know why we are here,' Sheikh interrupts one of the men on the other side, who won't stop talking.

'I assume but I will only speak for myself. I am tired of the fighting and of having soldiers insult our people in the name of protecting us. I don't want to have soldiers around my mosque. I am sure you don't want to have soldiers around your mosque. If we fight, it is Islam that suffers. Of course I don't agree with you and the things you practice. But is judgement not for Allah? Let us go to the heart of the matter and stop the accusations. And I will start by saying that I agree that we are at fault in the way in which it began. I am not joking about this. We accept the damage to the mosque and to your house and I am willing to pay restitution. I do not ask for anything in return. I do not seek retaliation or restitution, for my mosque or for getting shot. I do not even make any accusations. I just want the attacks to stop.'

The room is silent. Everyone, including the deputy governor, looks shocked. Even I am shocked. Sheikh leans back into his big cushion chair and rolls the beads on his chasbi. The Sultan has the same blank face he came with. For many minutes no one says anything. One by one, people lean back into their chairs, until no one is resting against their arms on the large round table except the woman writing what the deputy governor is saying and me.

'Shall we go for a short break?' the deputy governor proposes after a while.

'Ran ka ya dade, maybe not yet,' the Shiite malam says, 'I want to say something.'

Sheikh smiles.

'I see that all the arguments we brought have become useless. There is no longer any need to prove anything. If truly Sheikh means what he says, then this meeting will end earlier than we thought. And I thank him.'

'If not for the destiny of Allah which separated us, we might have been praying in the same mosque,' Sheikh says to the deputy governor, pointing at the Shiite malam. 'We used to play football together fa, only I was a much better player than he was.'

Everyone bursts into laughter, first nervously, then freely.

'On the issue of who was a better player, Sheikh, we might spend all night without a resolution,' the Shiite malam says.

The deputy governor is shaking his head and smiling. Everyone is.

'All that now remains, if you agree, is that the two of us, just the two of us this time, will have another meeting to discuss how we want to stop this from happening again and what exactly we need to do now to make sure that our people are on the same page with us.'

Sheikh agrees with the Shiite malam adding, 'Of course, if His Excellency and the Sultan agree, we can end this meeting and start one between us so that we can free him and his people.'

The deputy governor turns to the Sultan, who nods slightly.

'Alhamdulillah,' the deputy governor says. 'You may use our premises for as long as you want. I will not be far away. If you have reached a decision you can just call my PA and I will come down.'

We all take a break to eat and pray before Sheikh resumes alone with the Shiite malam. Everything is so large in Government House. The ceilings are so high, the tables so big and even the food in the dining room has chicken pieces so large I wonder if it is really chicken or turkey.

As one hour becomes two, I walk out to where the drivers are sitting under the shade of dogonyaro trees where they parked our cars. I lie down on one of the benches. It is cool here and there are many birds around. The flowers are trimmed and look so full and healthy.

When I close my eyes I see the smiling image of Aisha with her green veil and dimple on her right cheek. My mind replays our last meeting, when she gave me Sheikh's account details and smiled at me. I keep wondering if she just smiled or if she smiled at me. There must be a way of seeing her again.

The drivers are listening to a programme on BBC Hausa Service which mentions the war that ended in Gaza earlier this year. They are talking about how Israel is always looking for ways to kill all the Arabs there so the Israelis can take their land. One driver says that if he had the chance, he would go to Gaza and join Hamas just so he can kill an Israeli soldier. I want the meeting over so I can go and sleep.

Three hours later, Sheikh and the Shiite malam emerge from the office. They are both smiling and laughing and patting each other on the shoulder like they are friends just coming from watching a football game in a viewing centre.

Sheikh asks me to get the deputy governor's PA.

When the deputy governor arrives he shakes everyone's hand. The Shiite malam gives a summary of what they have agreed on. They will issue a joint statement to end the fighting and to pledge their commitment to peace. Neither of them will insult the other whether in sermons or otherwise. Sheikh will renovate the burnt Shiite mosque but not their malam's house, and the Shiites will pay for the books and equipment that got burnt since our mosque has already been renovated. Sheikh agrees. Malam Yunusa does not look too pleased.

The deputy governor talks about how happy he is that there is a resolution to the crisis and how the governor is committed to peace in the state. He talks for so long, I lose track of what he is saying and for a moment I stop writing.

The sultan speaks for the first time.

'I am here as an observer so I will not say much,' he begins, speaking slowly as if he is counting his words. I am dizzy looking at him and his big white turban. His outer robe has large patterns embroidered in gold thread. His face is clean: there is not a spot on it. There is neither a smile nor a frown on his face as he speaks and rolls the beads of his long white chasbi. It feels like he is not a human being. I almost forget that I need to write.

'I did not want to intervene when the matter became heated at first. It is important for all of you to come to an agreement by yourselves not pushed by me or by His Excellency. Now that we have reached a good conclusion, we can say it is your conclusion. Not ours. Peace is easier that way.'

There are photographers, who will take group pictures in front of the deputy governor's office. Sheikh asks me to stand by his side. My stomach is trembling just standing with all these men.

One of the men wearing a dark suit in the deputy governor's convoy takes off his large glasses momentarily and I see that he has one bad eye. He wipes his face with a handkerchief. The scar on his bad eye is unmistakable. I saw that scar every day when I was in Bayan Layi. He may be bigger and scarier but he is the same person I knew in Bayan Layi. I keep staring at him, trying to catch his eye, to see if he will recognise me. He keeps looking around with his mouth bunched like he was about to punch someone. I try to think of his name. I cannot remember calling him anything other than his street name. And I cannot just call out 'Acishuru.' He jogs with three others behind the deputy governor's car as it starts moving slowly until it picks up speed and zooms off. I wish I could stop him and ask about Gobedanisa and if they saw Banda's body after the police shot him. I wonder where I would be now if I did not run away from Bayan Layi.

Men from the deputy governor's office come to each of our convoys with big brown paper bags.

Sheikh asks what they are carrying.

'A gift from His Excellency,' the man says.

'Please open the bag.'

Sheikh peeps in it.

'Ah no!' Sheikh says. 'Not money, no. Please.'

The Shiite malam is looking at us from where his cars are parked.

He too refuses the bag he is given. The two men carrying the gifts walk away.

On our way back Malam Yunusa says, 'But Sheikh, forgive me if I say what I shouldn't, but haven't we conceded too much?'

'No we haven't.'

'But what of the mosque? And the car which was damaged when they attacked? Who will pay for that?'

'Malam Yunusa, the matter is not as simple as you see it. They did not attack me.'

'Haba? Then who did?'

'I do not want to sin by assuming. But I am sure that the Shiites are not the ones who shot me. When I am sure of it, I will tell you.'

'May Allah forbid evil.'

At the mosque, Sheikh asks me to organise the notes and give them to Sale to type and print out. Sale is one of the boys in our movement whom Sheikh had sent to the big computer school in town. He has now been employed as a typist.

'You, when will you learn how to use the computer, or do you want me to beg you?' Sheikh says to me as he walks out of his office.

'No, Sheikh. I will learn. I will ask Sale to teach me.'

'I want it all typed by evening tomorrow. You can go and rest now, but you must sit with him until he finishes typing.'

I nod.

When we began renovations after the attack on our mosque, the owner of one of the biggest computer stores in the market, who prays at our mosque, made a donation of a printer and two computers—one laptop and one desktop. I have seen computers in photocopying shops but I have never seen one this close.

I do not like Sale. His long bony fingers are always twirling matchsticks in his ears. I do not think he is smart at all. He stammers and, astaghfirullah, he reminds me of an earthworm with the way he does everything so sluggishly. I wonder how someone so sluggish and dull can learn to use something as complicated as a computer.

I wake up two hours later to the sound of an explosion and gunshots. I run out to see what is happening. People are running in the direction of the mosque. Some run past and some run in. The soldiers have gone crazy and are beating people randomly at the junction. A boy tells me that someone on a motorcycle tried to attack the checkpoint at the junction. The police shot him. No one knows who the man is.

Sheikh calls to ask if anything is going on in the mosque. I tell him everything is fine and that the commotion is at the junction.

'These fools want to spoil all of what we have achieved today. I have called everyone. Nothing happened in the mosque, so this is none of our business. We will carry on as if nothing happened. I don't even want people to gather and talk about it. Try and stay in if you can please. Don't go making enquiries that don't concern you.'

'OK, Sheikh,' I say.

I am worried about Jibril. I try his number. He has not been around since I came home. His phone is switched off. We must talk about this annoying habit of his when I see him; a phone should be kept on in case there is a problem and one needs to be reached. Otherwise what is the point of having a phone? I make my way to Malam Abdul-Nur's house, avoiding the main roads, where the policemen and soldiers are. Jibril goes there sometimes to run errands for his brother's wife or to eat food.

'Salamu alaikum,' I call out, standing in the zaure. There is no response. I am pushing the reed curtain aside to call out again, when I see the image of two people through the window across the courtyard. It is hard to make out what is happening. I know I shouldn't go in but I step closer and see Jibril, his hands in the air, trying to get into his caftan. A woman walks across, her hair uncovered, clutching a wrapper across her chest. I would not know what Malam Abdul-Nur's wife looked like if I saw her because she never steps out of the house. I walk back and stand outside the house.

Some minutes later Jibril walks out of the house. At first he is shocked to find me there but then he just turns away and continues walking.

'Why is your phone off?' I say angrily, trying to catch up with him.

He doesn't respond. I ask again and then he retorts, 'The battery died.'

'Don't go that way,' I say as he tries to turn onto the main road leading straight to the mosque. 'The soldiers have started harassing people. Somebody on a motorcycle threw a firebomb at the checkpoint. They shot him and then started harassing everybody.'

We walk in silence until we reach the mosque from the narrow path behind the motor park.

'What were you doing?' I ask as soon as we enter our room. I cannot hold it any longer.

'What do you mean what was I doing?'

'Don't lie to me Jibril, I am not a fool.'

'I went to run some errands.'

'Errands with your clothes off ko?'

'Who said I took my clothes off?'

'I saw you Jibril, stop lying! And I saw her too covering herself with a wrapper.'

He is grinding his teeth and staring into the ground. I sit on the bed right in front of him.

'Jibril?'

'Jibril!'

'Wallahi, you will not understand,' he says, his voice breaking.

'Understand what?'

I feel my own heart beating and my hands are shaking.

Many minutes pass. I do not know what to feel, what to say or if I should say anything. I start walking out of the room. Just when I am at the door, he starts.

'He treats her like a donkey.'

'What?' I pretend not to have heard him.

'Like a donkey. He treats her like an animal that he despises. Some days he locks her in her room without any food because his food is cold or there is too much salt or not enough salt. He beats her with a tyre whip. He forces things into . . .'

He stops. Tears start to flow and then he starts sobbing.

'He forces things into her . . . into her . . . anus! Candles. Bottles. He flogs her with the tyre whip when they are doing it. Some days she faints.'

I sit with him. I want to put my arm around his shoulders but I don't. All of a sudden I feel stupid for giving him such a hard time.

'Don't worry,' I say. 'It's not my business. I didn't see anything.'

He snuffles. The sound of his breath is heavy in the silence. It is hard to imagine both of them naked. I wonder what his face would look like, if he would look at her while he was doing it or if he would look away, if they would say anything to each other or just be quiet.

'Is it nice?' I ask.

'Yes,' he giggles, wiping his eyes. 'Very.'

OBSESS

1. Never stop thinking about something; to occupy somebodys thoughts constantly and exclusively.
2. Be preoccupied; to think or worry about something constantly and compulsively.

Aisha is in my heart like a spirit. When I close my eyes I see her. I open my eyes and any girl that is wearing a green hijab looks like her. She is the girl I am dreaming ~~Sometimes~~ of. Sometimes when she comes in the dream, her face is another persons face or sometimes she is not wearing green hijab. Sometimes she is not even wearing hijab at all and her body is like some of those bodys in EVERY WOMAN. Sometimes I wake up and I am sweating and my trouser is wet. Every time I wake up when my hand is almost touching her body.

    I think I am OBSESS.

WHY

Sometimes ~~a man~~ somebody is asking me why I am doing something or why I say something and I don't like it. Because it is not ~~all time~~ every time that ~~person~~ I will know the why. Sometimes you do something and it is only after that you think of the why. Sometimes there is no why. Like if somebody ask me why Aisha is making my chest to do somehow do I know? I just know that when I see her then I will feel something in my chest.

PART FOUR

A Taste of Haram

2010

When I read old magazines from outside Nigeria, I see how foreigners are always concerned with explaining things that have already happened. Everyone wants to tell you what someone was thinking, why someone did a thing, why someone said something. There is no way a person can know such things about another person. Allah alone knows the heart of a person. In the beginning, when I started reading, I too wanted to know why things happened. But time has taught me it is useless. Sometimes you let Allah do His things. What, apart from more unhappiness, is the use of trying to look into what only Allah knows and destines? Surely a man is happier just accepting the destiny of Allah.

But sometimes, astaghfirullah, I wish I could change some of the things that Allah has destined for us to do. I wonder if He also destines it when we engage in acts that are haram. Some things come back to you and you wish your life was like book and you could find that page in your life and tear it out.

Two months ago, not long after I found him with his brother's wife, Jibril asked me, as we went to buy a bag of rice for Sheikh, if I had ever slept with a woman. I wanted to lie to him that I had touched many girls in Bayan Layi the way I knew Banda and Gobedanisa did, but I couldn't lie to Jibril. There is a way he looks at me that makes lying difficult. Plus he tells me everything and I do not think that he lies to me. I know I might have touched girls if I had stayed a bit longer there.

'Let me take you to a place,' Jibril said.

'What place?'

'A place where you can meet women.'

'Haba Jibril. How do you know a place where there are women and I don't know the place.'

'It is because you do not want to know.'

'What if someone sees you?'

'That is why we will not use a microphone to tell the whole world we are going there ai.'

I looked around to make sure no one was listening.

'There are two places,' he began, 'one near mammy market and one behind the tipper garage.'

'What kind of women?'

'All sorts. Whichever you want. I have been there twice. The ones near mammy are more expensive because many people go there. But the ones behind tipper garage are cheaper.'

'Kai, Jibril, I am not sure about this.'

'When do you want to learn? Is it when you are married?'

'So you still go there even with her?'

His eyes dropped when I mentioned his brother's wife.

'I stopped going there when we started.'

'So you stopped and you want me to start ko?'

'Well you don't have anyone and I am not wanting you to do anything. I am only telling you there is a place. If you want, tell me and I will take you. Nobody is forcing you to do anything.'

He stood up and walked out of the room. I felt bad raising the issue of his brother's wife.

For two days I thought about this. On the third day, after countless dreams with all sorts of strange women, I spoke to Jibril right after maghrib prayers.

'How much do I need for that thing?'

'What thing?'

'The thing you said you would show me.'

'Which one of them?'

'The cheaper one.'

'Like five hundred for one hour.'

'Five hundred?'

'How much do you have?'

'Sheikh gave me three thousand to pay for his clothes with the tailor this evening and there is three hundred fifty change. I know he won't ask for it. But I want to give him anyway. I don't want him to start mistrusting me.'

'So, go to Sheikh now and give him the change. And if he says you can keep it, I will give you the remaining hundred fifty tomorrow.'

'What if he doesn't give me the change?'

'You worry too much. Go and ask first.'

Sheikh let me keep the change.

We went the next day after isha prayers. As we did not want anyone to see us or ask us where we were going, we did not take a motorcycle. We walked for a while, until we reached the tipper garage. Outside there were people with little kerosene lamps selling kolanuts and fried fish and suya and gurasa. Walking right through the darkness where the large trucks were resting for the night, we went past little red glows and people whispering in corners and open smelly gutters before bursting out onto a narrow street. From different small houses the music—Indian and Hausa—mixed with strong incense and tobacco came at us, strongly. Some of the women in front of the houses were standing alone, smoking, while others chatted with men.

'Babban yaya!' one girly voice called out to us from in front of a compound.

I turned to Jibril and he motioned with his head for us to go over. I grabbed him as I reluctantly made my way towards the voice.

'I don't bite. Come closer. Don't you want to see what you are buying?'

It made my stomach rumble that she could tell in the darkness that I was afraid. She had dark lips, a nose ring and a gold mecca tooth. Her scarf was halfway down her head, showing the front part of her curly hair. It was hard to tell if she was young or an older woman trying to look young.

Jibril got in front of me and held her hand which had black and red lalle patterns. I was shocked at how bold he was.

'My friend is looking for someone to give him a nice time.'

'The friend is dumb?'

'He has never . . .'

She smiled.

'Overnight or an hour?'

'An hour,' Jibril said.

He gave me a gentle push and said he would be waiting there when I finished.

'Switch off your phone,' he said, 'just in case they call you.'

The woman threw the gum she had been chewing in the waste bin in front of a room inside the compound. There were large posters of Indian actors as well as cutouts of naked white women. The bed was just a large mattress on the linoleum floor in the left corner. In the right corner was a table with a mirror, a kerosene lantern and a small clock.

'Do you want the light off or on?'

'Whatever,' I said.

'You need to relax or else you will not enjoy it. And you will still have to pay me for the hour.'

She dumped her clothes on the table and turned down the lantern. The dimness of the light seemed to have reduced the sounds wafting in from outside. I stared at her shadow on the wall.

'Help me,' she said, turning her back to me.

I struggled for a few seconds before unhooking her bra. She didn't complain. A bra is an interesting piece of clothing. I wonder who came up with the complicated idea.

My eyes followed the bra to the table.

'Take off your clothes.'

I find that the times that the rope of your trouser refuses to come undone are the times when you are desperate, like when you need to pee urgently. But when you don't need it to come undone, you have to keep tightening it.

'Can I see this?' I asked, pointing at the bra.

'Is this how you want to spend your hour or will you fuck me?' She threw the bra in my face.

I had never heard a woman use the phrase 'ci ni' before. Especially not a naked woman. It shocked and excited me all at once. Air seemed to leave the room and it became harder to breathe. My penis hardened into an erection, but my fingers still couldn't untie the knot.

'Have you been to Mecca before?' The words came out before I could stop them.

She hissed, snatched the bra and knelt down in front of me. She grabbed my penis through my trouser, first hard, then gently. Rising to her full height, she looked into my eyes as she stroked me with one hand and undid the knot with the other. As soon as it came loose and her hands touched my bare skin I felt it coming. I couldn't control it. Before she could push me onto the bed, I had ejaculated in her hands. She seemed upset at first, but then she smiled and got up to wipe her hands. I lay on the bed wishing that I could press a button and it would all be a dream.

'This really is your first time,' she said putting her bra back on.

'Please can we sit in a little? Just until the hour is up.'

I avoided her eyes as she crawled up to me on the bed. She put her arms around me.

'Don't worry. This will be our little secret. I won't tell your friend.'

'Thanks.'

'It will be better the next time. You just need to relax.'

I thought of Aisha. Her eyes were in every flicker of the low lantern flame. I thought of the man who asked during a tafsir if touching a woman without penetration is zina, trying to block out Sheikh's voice declaring any action that could lead to sex between unmarried people haram. In my head I felt shame, but in my heart I was glad I did not go all the way and actually commit zina.

We walked out together and met Jibril sitting on the culvert in front of the compound. I motioned with my head for us to leave.

'Your friend knows how to work o,' she said to Jibril as we walked away. His face broke into a proud smile. He patted me on the back. I tried to smile back.

'So tell me, what was it like? How was she?'

'It was good.'

'What do you mean it was good? I asked you to explain how it was, how she was.'

'Please, can we not talk about this?'

He laughed.

'Toh. Anyhow you want it.'

'So when are we coming back?' he added after a while.

'Never.'

He sighed. And we walked the rest of the way in silence.

ANTHROPOLOGY

1. The study of humankind, in particular.
2. (also cultural or social anthropology) The comparative study of human societies and cultures and their development.
3. (also physical anthropology) The science of human zoology, evolution and ecology.

In On the back of the new book, Baba of Karo, that Sheikh have allow me to open, it say that it is ANTHROPOLOGY. I have read almost to the end of the book and to me I am just thinking that it is a woman telling all the ~~story~~ stories of her life. I don't know why they have use the big word ANTHROPOLOGY when it is just a story.

I like the book but if it is me, I will call the book Life Story of Baba of Karo.

Maybe this Baba of Karo is telling lies or maybe it is old people of these days that is telling lies, I don't know. But every time old people is saying that before people is not doing bad bad things, that it is watching bad things on TV that is making people do bad things. But the bad things that Baba of Karo is writing that men and women are doing before before, I cannot even try it now. But maybe the old people don't want us to know the bad things they are doing when they are small.

I am happy that people are not catching other people as slaves the way Baba of Karo say they use to do before among Hausa people.

New Spaces

My dreams are strange. I dream that Sheikh has asked me to clear my things from my room in the mosque and move to one of Alhaji Usman's many blocks of flats. The house already has a bed, a cupboard, a fridge and a table and chair. Inside the compound where the house is, there are two three-bedroom flats and three two-bedroom flats. Then there is a little apartment that has a bedroom, a small parlour, a tiny kitchen and a toilet and bathroom. Just when I lie on the bed I wake up from the dream and I am in my room in the mosque. But then, I realise I am still dreaming. I wake up from that dream and discover that the first dream is actually real and that all the things I am dreaming about are actually true. The only difference is that in my dream the colour of the walls is different. It is hard to explain. I just don't believe it sometimes that all of this is real.

I cannot decide how best to arrange this room. This is the third time in a few weeks I am changing the position of the bed and the reading table. I think the bed right by the large window is best but I have been unable to sleep since I put the bed here. Thoughts of someone breaking in through the window and jumping onto my head or body make it difficult to sleep even though this bed is the best I have ever slept on. I have only ever slept on mattresses. Sometimes I am also scared I will roll over and fall onto the tiled floor.

I always thought, because of how Malam Abdul-Nur had a toilet inside his office, that I could never manage with the smell of shit inside a room, but I see now that having a toilet inside the room is not such a bad thing. All you need to do is close the door when you need to use the toilet. Using incense helps. I like the little pieces of wood soaked in essences from Maiduguri. Their incense is nicer than the cheap incense sticks from India, which make my chest hurt when I inhale a lot of the smoke. The toilet is narrow but everything in it is so white, sometimes I just go in there and sit down on the toilet seat to read an old magazine. On the right side, divided by a plastic curtain, is the shower.

I had come with nails thinking that I would need to hang a few things on the wall. But taking one look at the smooth, clean walls, I knew I could not bring myself to use nails. Moreover the cupboard has space for everything I have.

Sometimes I feel like I chose the wrong colour for this room. Sheikh had asked me when they were renovating the apartment before I moved in. White gets dirty easily. It is the same reason I am always afraid to wear a white caftan. You wear it once and by evening it is already dirty. Jibril likes to lie on the bed and suspend his legs on the wall. Every time, this leaves stains and when I tell him he gets upset and doesn't come back or call me for two days. But I like

Jibril. He doesn't stay upset for too long. Good thing is, the walls are so smooth you can use a rag soaked in detergent to wipe off the dirt.

Going through my old newspapers, I stumble on that piece of paper with the phone number my brothers left behind when they disappeared. I stare at the paper so long, I start to see their faces. The faces are not the faces of people I know, who grew up with me in the same house. I want to call but I do not know what to say.

It is 9 p.m. when I hear the knock on my door. I realise it is Sheikh when he calls out my name. The room is a mess and I scramble to put things in order.

'Salamu alaikum,' I say to him as I open the door.

'I have bothered you, ko?'

'Ah, Sheikh, how can you bother me? You can never bother me.'

'Why does the whole place smell like this?'

'It is from the kitchen, Sheikh. I bought a new stove.'

'A new stove? To set the house on fire?'

He laughs and pulls his grey beard.

'I was cooking Indomie.'

'Burning Indomie, you mean.'

I laugh and offer him a chair.

Since the shooting, his wrinkles and the grey hairs on his head have multiplied. He looks around the room and asks if I like the house. This is the first time he has come here since I moved. The place is perfect, I tell him. The only problem was the lock on the front door, which I have had changed. There is an expression in his eyes, the look of one with something heavy or unpleasant to say. He rolls his prayer beads.

'Allah has blessed us,' he begins. 'A while back when I first mentioned the movement, people thought I was crazy. Now we have thousands of members and everyone wants me to do something for them. They all come under the cover of night to my house—commissioners, even the deputy governor. The last money I sent you to deposit—that was from him.'

He pauses and clears his throat.

'But that is not why I am here. Sometimes we get carried away. I want to ask you a favour. These people around me, apart from Malam Yunusa, I don't expect them to tell me the truth. They are all too loyal. Loyalty is good, but I want someone who thinks too. That is why despite all Malam Abdul-Nur's atrocities I kept him. His thoughts may sometimes be evil, but he thinks. And for a while he kept everyone in line. It is he who organised most things around here. He knows how to organise. But you, I want to ask from you one thing. Tell me what you do not like or understand. Anything. I know you are loyal. But I also know that you think.'

My heart is beating so loud it feels like he must hear it. I do not want to think that he is testing me. Sheikh is not one to test a person.

'Ya Sheikh, you have been kind and good to me . . .'

'No, Ahmad,' he interrupts, 'I do not want to hear about my kindness and goodness. Tell me about my badness and about the things that worry you. Talk to me. Man to man. Tonight there will be no preaching. Only talking, man to man. Tonight I am just your friend.'

'OK, Sheikh. Maybe the biggest issue in my mind is the money. Why do you take money from these people? Also, why have you kept Malam Abdul-Nur close? I know you have explained that, but I still don't understand. Allah forgive me, but he is not a nice person.'

'Good. I see our relationship will last long. The money. About the money. When I first started, I used to reject money. All of it. Even from Alhaji Usman. But you know what I have learned, Ahmad? Poverty does not make a man decent. Poverty is not piety. In the same vein, money does not make a man evil. A man's character is not defined by what money he has or does not have, but what decisions he takes in spite of having or not having. There are people who have lived a life of abject poverty who will be the first at the gates of hell. But even now there are people whose money I cannot accept because they tie obligations to it. I can take your money, but you will never control me. If Alhaji Usman were to do something I thought was evil today, I would be the first to condemn it.'

He starts to cough, first gently then wildly. I fetch some water for him to drink. He coughs a little more before it stops.

'And as for Abdul-Nur, our history is long. When I was a teacher at the College of Islamic Studies I went for a conference of Islamic Studies teachers in Ilorin. On the last day of the conference I was so fed up with the town and didn't want to sleep in Ilorin even though it was late. On the way, just outside Ilorin our vehicle had a flat tire and we were attacked by some armed robbers. I got a knife wound and we all ran into the bush. I bled so much, I fainted. It was Malam Abdul-Nur who found me and took me into his house and they called someone to treat me with herbs until I got better. All the while everyone thought I was dead. It is Allah who destines all things but I could have died if it was not for Malam Abdul-Nur. I was in that village for one week. And as we kept in touch, we argued about Christianity and Islam until I convinced him that Islam was the right way. You see, it is hard to let go of such a person.'

I have never seen Sheikh like this. It is like something has been loosened within him, like he has stripped his skin to let me see the blood that flows beneath it.

'I know,' he continues, 'I know that he sometimes takes our money. I know what he thinks about jihad. If you let him, he would attack this minute. But I try to keep him in check and let Allah judge him. I think in all of this, his heart is still good.'

I sigh and sip some water.

'Do you have any more questions?'

'Nothing else comes to mind, Sheikh.'

'But promise me that if you are uncomfortable with any-thing, you will tell me.'

'I will, Sheikh, I promise.'

'We need to do something about you trying to burn down this house, eh?'

I laugh. He gets up to leave.

'Seriously, Ahmad, this cooking business is not for you. I will ask them to keep a portion of food for you every evening. Just drop your food flask in the morning and pick it up in the evening.'

'Ah, thank you, Sheikh.'

He smiles and as he walks out the door he says, 'I cannot have an unmarried deputy, you must think about this and tell me if there is anyone in your mind, otherwise we can arrange something for you. You are young, but you are mature enough to marry. The earlier the better.'

I walk him out of the gate. His two guards are sitting on the pavement and get up as soon as I open the gate.

'Think seriously about it,' he says as he walks away.

Just after the early morning prayers, I am sitting in Sheikh's office reading a *Daily Trust* newspaper from last week. I do not know why every newspaper needs to have a sport section. It annoys me to hear boys who can barely afford to eat fight over Arsenal and Manchester and Real Madrid. Does any one of those footballers or clubs even know they exist? Sometimes, especially when boys gather behind the mosque in the morning, arguing about which club is better, I want to come out and just pour cold water on their bodies. This is the one thing I cannot stand about Jibril: he loves everything about football. He knows the names of all the players and how much each of them earns. He has a huge stack of sports newspapers, which he buys without fail. I know that when he asks me for fifty naira, that is what he wants to buy. I have told him that I can give him anything except for money to buy sports papers.

People are shouting right behind the window of Sheikh's office—they do this especially when Sheikh is not around. The commotion is getting louder and I walk out to see what it is. As I approach, I see boys in a circle around two people. I move closer and see that it is Jibril squeezing someone's neck inside his arm and giving head butts. The other person is struggling, trying to use his knee to hit him in the stomach.

'Kai! Kai! Kai!' I scream, running through the circle.

'Jibril! Jibril! Leave him,' I scream, pulling his right arm. The other person is one of Sheikh's new bus drivers in the motor park. Jibril's grip is too firm. I get a stick and whip them both on the legs and back. They both let go and the driver falls to the ground; his eyes and lips are swollen and blood trickles from his nostrils. Jibril has bite marks on his right arm.

The driver is panting and shouting, 'Bastard! Infidel! Stupid infidel! Offspring of an infidel!'

I walk over angrily and whip him three times on the back, until he stops screaming. Jibril points at him and says, 'Next time I will kill you!' I slap Jibril across the cheeks and just when he opens his mouth to complain, I slap him again, then drag him by the arm, away from the crowd. Everyone is silent and people begin to disperse.

'Are you crazy?' I ask as soon as we get into the room. 'Do you see what you did to his face? What will I tell Sheikh now? That you blinded his driver?'

'You heard what he was calling me! You heard him!'

'So what? So what if he insulted you? Do we go blinding everyone who says something bad to us?'

He lowers his head, wiping the blood on his body with his torn caftan. I take a look at his bite marks. They are deep and ugly.

'You should go and let Chuks treat those wounds.'

He throws the torn, bloody caftan on the ground and picks up the plastic kettle from the side of his mattress.

'I am sorry I slapped you so hard. You know that if I hit only him, they will say that I was siding with you.'

He puts on his slippers and leaves the room. I walk out after him to look for the driver who was hurt. I find him sitting against a tree, with four boys talking and observing his wounds.

'You need to go and have your wounds treated,' I tell him.

'Chuks has not opened yet,' he slurs.

'Go into the compound. He has his room there. He will come out. Don't worry, I will pay for it. It will not be more than two or three hundred.'

'Thank you.'

'Don't thank me. You should know better than to call a Muslim an infidel.'

'It was what he was saying. He was supporting America. He was saying Osama should not have attacked America. That Osama caused the world to start hating Muslims.'

'Is Osama your brother? Are you the one who sent him? Are you the one who decides who is an infidel and who is not? You have become Allah, no?'

The other boys are grumbling and mumbling things I cannot hear.

'What did you say?' I ask one of the boys mumbling.

'Nothing,' he says, turning away.

After the zuhr prayer I stare at the piece of paper with my brothers' phone number again. I dial and stop it twice before finally letting it ring.

'Salamu alaikum. Who is speaking?' It is Hussein's soft voice.

'It is me, Ahmad.'

'Ahmad?'

'Dantala.'

'Oh, sorry. Dantala, how are you doing?'

'Fine. Why are you whispering?'

'I am in the hospital. Maccido is injured. Soldiers shot at them last night.'

'La ila ha illallah! How is he?'

'I don't know. They are trying to remove the bullets in his shoulder and arms.'

'Where are you, what town? I can travel to wherever you people are.'

'You don't have to come, Dantala.'

'Are you crazy? What do you mean I don't have to come? Where are you?'

'General. General Hospital here in Sokoto.'

'In Sokoto? I didn't know you were here. I thought you were in Zaria.'

'No. We came to Sokoto.'

'Anyway, I am coming now.'

I head for Sheikh's office. I am tired in my body and in my head. Sokoto was not like this before. We used to hear of these things in Jos and Kaduna and Kano. It used to be as distant as the car bombs in Iraq and Lebanon. It didn't mean anything to me because this place was always peaceful.

At Sheikh's office I see Alhaji Usman's car. In the office Alhaji Usman is leaning against the window with his hands over his face. Sheikh is on the phone pleading with someone.

'It is his son fa, think if it was your own son, haba Mohammed,' Sheikh says.

Sheikh walks out into the open yard. I feel very awkward seeing Alhaji Usman like this. When Sheikh returns about ten minutes later he says to Alhaji Usman: 'He has agreed. Let us go.' He asks me to follow them. They are going to the hospital morgue, where they will meet with the big Shiite malam to collect the corpse of Alhaji Usman's son who died last night. The Shiites wanted to bury him because he was one of them and had been living with them. Alhaji Usman wanted his son's body.

'What did you come to tell me?' Sheikh asks as we drive out in Alhaji Usman's jeep.

'My brother was shot last night and he is in the hospital.'

'Another shooting?' Sheikh cries out.

'Where is he?'

'General Hospital.'

'OK, well we are going to the morgue of the General Hospital too.'

Sheikh makes three other calls in the car. He calls the head of the drivers in the motor park to meet him at the morgue, the grave digger to start digging the grave, and the deputy governor to inform him that the time for the funeral is 3 p.m.

'What did I do?' Alhaji Usman whispers. 'What wrong did I ever do?'

'It's OK, Alhaji,' Sheikh says.

'They said I should take it easy with him. I took it easy. He became worse. They said I should be stricter. He moved out and ran away.'

The new smell of this car is making my nose tingle. I sneeze.

'Yar Hamoo Kallah,' everyone says.

'Did you say your brother was shot?' Alhaji Usman asks, just realising I had said this five minutes ago.

'Yes,' I reply.

'What is this country turning into? Sheikh, what are we going to do about this?'

'Don't worry,' Sheikh says, 'you just worry about the funeral.'

At the hospital Sheikh pulls the big Shiite malam to the side and they have a long talk. Everyone watches them intently. They walk back and go into the morgue alone. Sheikh calls out to Alhaji Usman. He follows them. I call Hussein again. He says that they have finished the procedure and that

Maccido is sleeping. I ask if he has seen him and he says no. He tells me which ward they are in.

The Shiite malam comes out first and together with his people they walk towards the main hospital complex. Sheikh comes out with Alhaji Usman, who is wiping his face. They talk to the morgue attendant and Alhaji Usman begins filling out some forms.

I walk with Sheikh and we ask where the Accidents and Emergencies ward is. When we get in, the Shiite malam is there talking to Hussein and a few other men.

'We meet again,' the Shiite malam says, 'do you have a patient here?'

'It is my deputy, whose brother is here. He was shot by soldiers.'

'What is his name?'

'Maccido,' I reply, 'Hussein is my brother too.'

They all stare in amazement.

'I knew his siblings were Shiites but I didn't know they were your boys,' Sheikh says to the Shiite malam.

'How small the world is. How small it is!'

'We need to meet with a few of the other malams because it seems we have common problems,' Sheikh says.

I learn from Hussein that they were all in the same private bus when the soldiers harassed them last night. Alhaji Usman's son Al-Amin was driving and Maccido was sitting in the back. A soldier slapped Al-Amin for not turning off the engine when they stopped. They were asked to all get out of the bus and they refused. The soldier shot through the door, wounding Al-Amin in the hip. He started the bus and drove off. The soldiers fired a few more shots, which wounded Maccido and one other man sitting in front. Al-Amin didn't stop driving until they got to the mosque, where he fainted. At the hospital, the nurses tried in vain to stop the bleeding. There was no doctor available that night and by the morning, when the Shiite malam was able to get a doctor he knew personally, Al-Amin was dead.

This is all too much for me. Fear and anger and sadness and tiredness are competing for space in my body. I feel like I have lost weight in just these few hours. The doctors are not letting anyone see Maccido yet. Perhaps tomorrow I will be able to go in.

Hussein comes with us to Al-Amin's funeral. He does not say anything to me.

After the prayers, Sheikh and the Shiite malam speak to the crowd. While the Shiite malam is speaking, Sheikh whispers to me.

'We are marching to Government House to demonstrate about this. You must go back to the mosque and stay there.'

'I want to come too,' I protest.

'The Americans, do you know that the president and vice president never travel together in the same plane? Do you know why?'

I shake my head.

'Someone has to take over in case something happens to one person, no?' He pauses and then adds, 'Sometimes you steal lessons even from the infidel. Go. Now.'

I push through the crowd. Jibril is standing behind, stretching to see what is going on in front. With my eyes I tell him to follow me. We walk away from the burial ground, our feet unconsciously moving at the same pace. We take the shortcuts we both know well, jumping open gutters, squeezing through very narrow spaces between mud houses, bursting into the open football field belonging to the government primary school and then behind the land which is now a maize farm opposite our mosque. I look at the slight swelling on his head and ask if Chuks treated his bites. He nods.

In the mosque I ask for Jibril's radio. He says he forgot it in his brother's house. I tell him that he has to be careful. He shows me some pills and says he got them from Chuks.

'She cannot get pregnant,' he whispers.

'Are you crazy? What if this hurts her?'

'Hold on now,' he says trying to get me to lower my voice, 'she has been using it before we started.'

'I don't understand.'

'Since he started beating her and she lost one pregnancy, she swore that as long as he was beating her she would never get pregnant for him.'

'She lost one pregnancy?'

'Yes. You know she was pregnant when I first came. That one she gave birth to dead. It was the second one she lost when he was beating her.'

'I didn't hear of this at all.'

'Yes, he didn't tell anyone. He just called her sister, who works as a cleaner in a hospital in Ilorin. Her sister took care of her until she got better. He didn't want anyone to know. It was the sister who suggested the pills and got them for her.'

'You just be careful fa!'

I lie down and doze off until Sheikh and all the others return just in time for maghrib. I ask Sheikh how it all went and he tells me the governor came out to see them and begged them not to act in anger.

'But of course you know politicians,' he says. 'He saw our numbers and the only thing he didn't promise was aljanna firdaus.'

He has eye bags like someone who hasn't slept in days.

'What of the soldiers who shot them?' I ask.

'I am told they redeployed them yesterday. But we have a meeting with the head of the Task Force tomorrow. You will come with me.'

'What time Sheikh?'

'They will call to confirm, but it will be after isha, insha Allah. Have you called again about your brother?'

'Yes, he is OK.'

'Well, Alhamdulillah. Don't forget to collect food from my house. I told them you will start coming to collect food'

I do not know why I lied. I could have just said I have not called Hussein since I left. The words just came out as lies. Is this the sign of being a bad person, lying without even thinking it?

I call Hussein. He tells me Maccido has woken up and they have just spoken. Maccido will be fine, he says.

It is just after isha and I am waiting inside the zaure of Sheikh's house. A little boy has gone into the house to tell them that I am outside. Less than a minute later, the boy runs out.

'They said they are coming,' he says and starts to run off.

'You didn't wait to collect the food for me,' I shout as he runs down the road, not even turning to listen to me.

The house has been renovated recently with a new large gate like the new houses in town and the compound I live in. But the house still has a zaure like the older houses.

'Salamu alaikum,' Aisha says stretching out the food warmer.

'Salamu alaikum wa rahmatullahi wa barakatuh,' I reply wiping my hands behind my thighs.

I don't know why I am wiping my hands or why suddenly it is hard for me to breathe.

'Thank you. What is it?'

'Yam and eggs.'

'Please forgive me,' I blurt, 'but I keep wondering if you have any hijabs that aren't green.'

'What does that mean?' She sounds upset.

'Well I have only seen you wear green and now you are wearing green.'

'How many times have we met?'

I pretend I do not know exactly how many times I have seen her.

'Maybe three or four times?'

'So three times is enough to know all a person's clothes?'

'That's not what I mean,' I start to say before she turns and says, 'I leave you well.'

I have that feeling again. Of wanting to step out of my body and slap myself really hard and watch myself scream in pain because of how stupid I have just been.

FAMILIAL

1. Common to families: of or relating to a family

When I first read this word in a newspaper, I am thinking it is another way of spelling FAMILIAR.

Now that all of my brothers that remain are in this same Sokoto, I don't know if I am happy or if I am not happy. I am asking myself if there is something that is the same in all families like something that all families must do. Something like liking each other. I know that Jibril does not like his brother. But it is because his brother likes to beat and wound people. Me, I don't know why I am feeling like this about my brothers. I am not feeling like and I am not feeling hate. I am feeling as if they are just some people that we entered the same bus with, people you will forget when you drop from the bus. Allah forgive me.

DERBY

1. an annual horse race run on the flat at Epsom
2. a similar race held elsewhere
3. Local Derby: a football match between two teams from the same district or area.

I am always seeing Derby in Jibril football newspaper that he like to buy every time. Sometime I am thinking of Malam Abdul-Nur sermon when he talk of why football and going to viewing centre to watch football is haram. I don't like football. I know that to be mixing with men and women in the ~~staduim~~ stadium and the betting that some people use to do for football is haram. But is buying the football newspaper haram? And me that is looking at the one that Jibril is buying, am I doing haram? I don't want to ask Sheikh or Malam because maybe they will know that somebody is buying the newspaper and Jibril will not be happy if I ask.

Cholera

Since the cholera outbreak in many villages, our movement has been supporting the volunteers going round talking to people about open defecation, hand washing, boiling or purifying water and washing fruits and vegetables thoroughly before eating. A lot of people have died and relief from the state and local government either takes forever to come or doesn't come at all. The first time it happened the local government chairman came around with some materials and a lot of cameramen. I thought they would return but it was all a show. Movements like ours and the Dariqas and the Shiites are coming in to help with clean water, drugs and burying the dead.

Sale designed the images which we took to have printed on big polythene sachets with the name of our movement and logo and the logo of Islamic Relief in England, which sends us water purifiers. Sheikh gave me eight hundred thousand naira to fill two thousand sachets with soap, rice and oral rehydration salts. We will add one water purifier and two hundred naira in each sachet. About half of the sachets are for our members and the remaining we will distribute to others. There are also leaflets in Hausa about how to maintain hygiene and what to do when someone starts vomiting or stooling. I don't know how many people can read Hausa.

Sale is crunching fresh tiger nuts, pouring the chaff on the table. He chews like that prostitute I met behind the tipper garage.

'Sale, you shouldn't leave that thing lying there, look at all the flies,' I tell him.

'I will pack it,' he says, his mouth full.

'No,' I say, 'clear it now. I don't want flies in this place. This is how cholera starts.'

Slowly, he spits out the chaff from his mouth into his hand and puts it in an old polythene bag. Astaghfirullah, but I don't know why people like him don't get cholera.

'Flies will still follow the bag, so tie it.'

He wipes his hand on his clothes and ties the polythene bag. I find that since the day I broke up the fight between Jibril and the driver, no one even tries to challenge me around here. It is interesting that it is not Sheikh saying I am his deputy that has made people respect me but me flogging and slapping two grown people in public. I think that is why Malam Abdul-Nur had so many people following him. He never hesitated to hit or slap. I don't understand people.

I am with two volunteers on the way to the first village outside Sokoto city to deliver relief materials: two hundred sachets and a hundred bags of pure water. We are using a new Hilux truck, which was donated by Islamic Relief and has the same driver who fought with Jibril.

Travelling in this truck is better than using the buses especially because of the areas with bad roads. You don't feel the bumps so much. Also the radio has really clear speakers and doesn't give me a headache.

Everyone must be tired from packing and sealing sachets last night. We haven't even been travelling for thirty minutes and apart from the driver and me, everyone is dozing off.

The village looks deserted. But for two old men tilling a farm and two children rolling old bicycle tyres, we meet no one on our way to the village head's house. He has already lost one of his wives and one of his daughters to cholera. He takes us round the village as we distribute the items and talk to people about hygiene. At the home of one of our members we drop ten bags for him to share with other members we cannot meet. We do not let the village head see this.

On our way back to the village head's house, we hear screaming. We stop and follow the sound until we find the house where it is coming from. We say salaam and enter. There are two men, one young and the other older, on the floor, covered in flies, emaciated and barely breathing. Two women are kneeling over them, wailing.

'It is cholera,' one of the volunteers says.

He goes back to the truck and gets gloves and face masks. The volunteers ask us to step aside and they carry the men out one by one and put them into the back of the truck. They prepare two oral rehydration salt mixtures and ask the women to make the men drink these as we begin to make our way to the health centre close to the city. The village head leaves us and bids us goodbye.

I cannot stop turning to look at the men in the back of the truck. They are throwing up as the women make them drink the solutions. This is the first time I am this close to someone who has cholera. There are tears in the driver's eyes. We almost run a goat over as we reach the main road. The driver looks at me like he expects me to tell him to slow down. I don't tell him anything.

By the time we have got to the health centre, the young man is no longer breathing. Two attendants come and take the two men and lay them on mats outside the building because there are no beds. They take the young man away to the back where they keep dead bodies. We stay at the health centre for thirty minutes while they try to get the only doctor to come around. The older man is throwing up and stooling at the same time. His eyes begin to go pale.

When the doctor comes, he feels the man's pulse and shakes his head. The doctor looks like he is going to collapse himself. When the attendants come to take the man's body, the two women resume wailing.

I walk to a tree away from the health centre, squat and let my tears flow.

Revelations

It has been four months since Malam Abdul-Nur returned from Saudi Arabia with a turban and a new movement in opposition to Sheikh. It feels like four years with how popular he is, especially among motorcyclists, tea sellers and butchers. No one knows how he got all the money he used to set up his foundation. And no one is asking. All we know is suddenly there are black-and-white banners, flags and stickers everywhere that read either 'Mujahideen' or 'Sunna Sak.'

Many of the young people who used to be with us now follow Malam Abdul-Nur. They have left the open arms of Sheikh and fallen under the strict hand of the new leader of Firqatul Mujahideen li Ihyau Islam, who I hear has organised them into units and teams. Each unit is made up of fifty people and each team is made up of five units with a team leader. The team leader collects taxes from the unit leaders and people can receive loans to start new businesses or expand old ones.

A few weeks ago they had a clash with the police. Up to two policemen and ten of their members died. They beat up anyone who tries to make trouble with them and they threaten nonmembers who have similar businesses around them.

Malam Abdul-Nur now preaches openly against us, mentioning us by name, mocking us in his sermons. Last month Malam Abdul-Nur challenged Sheikh to a doctrinal debate about whether it is haram to go to university and work for the government. Sheikh agreed. They decided to do it in Saudi Arabia, where they were both travelling, away from the distraction of screaming followers. Sheikh had the debate taped and the CD was just delivered to us by post. He has asked me to arrange for it to be played in the school.

Even our school has taken a massive hit. Many of our older male students have dropped out and act as thugs for Malam Abdul-Nur. I am not sure if it is the hope of money that lures them or the fact that the Mujahideen movement is something new. Everyone likes something new. Eventually people get tired and some other new thing takes over. It isn't grounded. Something that has no roots and springs up with leaves and branches everywhere is bound to crash from the weight. They can't see this now. But soon they will understand their mistake. At the last meeting we had with Sheikh, Alhaji Usman and the other trustees, we agreed that as long as Malam Abdul-Nur was not harassing or attacking any of our people, we would just watch and see how things turn out.

Sale doesn't work on Saturdays. This is a source of great relief to me as I open Sheikh's former office in the mosque to rest before I call the zuhr prayers. I still call it Sheikh's office even though it is now mine. I still see myself as a visitor especially because of the big shelf that has all of his books.

Just before I push open the office door, I look to the right and see a key in the keyhole of Jibril's door. He is hardly ever here these days but he still keeps the key. Since Malam Abdul-Nur started his Mujahideen movement, Jibril comes in only after maghrib prayers. I thought Sheikh would object to Jibril still using that room but Sheikh told him that as long as he wants to keep coming back, he will be welcome.

I open the door and on the bare bed is a sheet of paper with my name. I dial Jibril's number and it is switched off.

'I have packed to stay with my brother,' the note begins. 'I will still try to come and see you. I didn't want to go but you know how my brother is. He doesn't even want to see me around this area. Please apologise to Sheikh for me. Don't try to come and look for me. It will put me in trouble.'

My eyes cannot focus on the book I am reading because of this headache. I haven't had any food since last night. When I step out, the sun is so hot I feel like turning back and sending one of the boys in the mosque to get some food for me from Sheikh's house. But the reward of seeing Aisha is worth being burnt by the sun.

It is not Aisha, but Zulfau, her sister, who brings out the food flask and hands it to me looking away.

'What of Aisha?' I ask.

'She is not around,' Zulfau says, and starts walking back in.

'Where is she?'

She turns into the house without even looking back. I peep in and see Aisha walking past.

'Aisha!' I call out.

She quickens her pace and disappears into the compound. It feels like being sliced in the heart with a butcher's sharp knife. I walk out into the street feeling the sun even hotter than when I set out.

Black smoke is rising in the distance. I can hear the chants of a crowd. I should just head to the mosque but I turn off the road in the direction of the smoke and the screaming. I see a boy coming from there and ask what is going on.

'They are burning books,' he says.

'Who is burning books?'

'It is the Mujahideen people.' He wants to add something but looks at me suspiciously.

'What is it?'

'Our malam says they are infidels led by a convert who is trying to lead Muslims astray.'

'Who is your malam?'

'Malam Mohammed Sani.'

Mohammed Sani is one of the new dariqa malams. He was a student of Abduljalal, whom Sheikh often had heated but friendly debates with. He disagrees with us but we always get along fine. Sometimes during Ramadan we all break fast together.

I reach the source of the smoke and find a huge crowd. People are throwing books and papers into the fire. Malam Abdul-Nur is supervising the burning, adding kerosene any time the items being dumped seem to be overwhelming the fire. Every time the flames leap from the pile the crowd screams: 'Allahu Akbar!' There is excitement on their faces and many are jumping and pumping their fists in the air. Malam Abdul-Nur has told them that before they can truly join his movement they must burn any school certificates they have. They are also burning the books by Hausa writers because those books corrupt women with tales of illicit love affairs. And they are burning CDs of Hausa movies, which he says are products of Kano, a city of corrupt wealth, usury and decadence.

They are burning things with so much zeal, if Malam Abdul-Nur sees me spying on them he just might throw me in the fire. I leave before anyone recognises me.

I don't know if asking Sale to teach me how to use the computer makes him instantly hungry or if he just doesn't like me. As soon as I come for my lessons, he remembers that he needs to go to Saudatu and makes me wait until he slurps his way through his koko or munches on kosai and bread. He never offers; he just makes me sit through the whole process. And I hate the smell of food if I am not eating it. I have tried coming at different times of the day, but it is always the same.

Perhaps he thinks I will get tired or upset and stop coming. I don't care really. Once I learn enough, I will tell him my thoughts about his behaviour. But then Umma used to say that sometimes the people we call wicked are just foolish and that, while it is easy to repent being wicked, it is hard to stop being foolish.

I need to get my head around Microsoft Excel. Even with the many commands I have to learn, Microsoft Word is easy. Excel is so complicated it gives me a headache, the kind that makes the right side of my head throb with pain. At least I can practice alone when Sale is gone for the day.

Jibril's eyes are swollen and red. They have been this way for the past week during which we have been secretly meeting behind Sheikh's millet farm. Every day I ask what is wrong, he says it is nothing. Now he is gritting and grinding his teeth and breathing hard.

'I have to move again,' he says.

'Where to now?'

'I don't know. He has bought a huge farm outside the city and he is moving away with all his people. They have just finished building his own house and many tents around, where the people will stay. The farm is in quite a remote place. I have never gone, but they say it is like three hours away from the border. He is calling it the hijra.'

'Is that why you look so ill?'

'I have not been sleeping,' he admits finally.

'Because you are leaving?'

'No, something else.'

'What is it? Do you want me to beg you? I have been asking you for days now.'

'She is pregnant,' he whispers.

'She is pregnant! Pregnant?'

He nods.

'How did this happen. I thought you said she was taking those pills.'

'I think the pills we got from Chuks didn't work.'

'Trouble! Kai! I told you to be careful, Jibril!'

'She says that she discovered one month ago. But she says that after that he has slept with her at least twice so there is no way of him discovering that it is not his. Honestly, I am worried. He will kill me if he finds out. Now she wants to tell him that she is pregnant.'

'Then don't go with him, Jibril.'

'I don't want to leave her.'

I want to slap his mouth.

'What do you mean?'

'I like her.'

'You like her? To sleep with her is one thing, now you like her?'

'Yes.'

'What does that mean? You want her? You want to marry her? What?'

'I just like her.'

'You are crazy!'

'I know.'

As he turns to leave he says to me, 'Will you forgive me if I tell you something?'

'Kai, what can be worse than this, Jibril?'

'Just say you will forgive me.'

'I will forgive you.'

'You remember when there was the fight about who put an X on the mosque?'

'Yes?'

'It was me who painted it. He asked me to do it. I didn't know why but he made me swear not to tell anyone.'

'It's OK,' I say. But I am angry at him for making me keep all these heavy secrets. I walk away before he tells me anything worse.

This is the first time people will be seeing the debate. I had advised Sheikh to hold off the distribution of the free CDs until after we show it on a projector. Everyone inside our school premises is helping out, arranging chairs and mats and weeding the grasses that have grown beside the football field. Sheikh has asked everyone to let their wives come out and watch the video. The women will sit in the opposite direction with their own screen, separated by a wall of white cloth suspended by two iron rods. I do not understand how this will work but the man setting up the projector has assured me that they will see and hear the exact same thing. The armed policemen that will stand guard together with our boys from our newly formed volunteer guard have already arrived. They came in two vans with eight men each. I greet their leader and ask them if they need anything.

'My boys are thirsty. They have not drank anything since morning,' the man with a huge belly and a rifle hanging from his shoulder says.

'Give me ten minutes,' I tell them.

I ask one of the boys who came with his motorcycle to take me to Sheikh's house, where food and drinks are being prepared. I hope that at least some of the snacks are ready so I can add them to the drinks.

'They are making zobo, ginger and kunu,' Aisha tells me when she meets me in the zaure. There is so much noise coming from inside the house with all the women who have volunteered to help cook.

'Salamu alaikum,' Aisha says.

'Wa alaikum wassalam. Two days. One never sees you.'

'Yes. They say, "Eye, who do you take for granted? The one who you see often."'

I laugh. I ask for sixteen packs of snacks and a mix of all three drinks together with water.

'Did you come with a bus?' she asks.

'No,' I say, 'we came with a motorcycle.'

'Then how are you going to carry all these things? Sheikh also wants you to go with some of the CDs so you can lock them up in one of the classrooms or in his office.'

'Don't worry, I will go with the food and come back,' I say and smile at her.

She shakes her head and mumbles, 'Men though! Why go through all that trouble?'

She counts sixteen sachets of water and a mix of sixteen sachets of other drinks in separate polythene bags.

'All we have now is the meat and masa,' she says.

'That's fine,' I say.

She is not wearing a full hijab and neither is she wearing green. I want to tease her but there is already a big frown on her face from having to cook all day and she might not find it funny.

'You need to call before you come back or send someone to come back so we can get everything ready for you to just take.'

'I can only call if I have your number,' I say to her.

'You mean you don't have my number?'

'You never gave it to me.'

She mumbles something and starts to call out her number.

The policemen are excited that they have a lot to eat and drink. I worry at how it only takes a few sachets of zobo and meat for them to start calling me oga. But for their guns, they all look useless. The boys of our volunteer guard are smarter than these men.

I call Yushau, who was recently chosen by Sheikh to head the volunteer guard, and tell him to be extra vigilant because these policemen look like they came for the zobo and whatever cash we will give them before they leave. I like Yushau. He is very stern and takes his job almost too seriously. But he is a very humble person. He keeps all the boys in line and never complains about anything. Sometimes I want to tell him to relax and that this is not a real army but I like his zeal.

I wish Jibril were here to help me organise things. He no longer uses the same number and although he has called me twice with a new one he has asked me not to call him because his brother would get suspicious and ask who it is. He is afraid of everything around him. He tells me it is all like an army training camp. In the new compound, where he lives, far outside the city, Malam Abdul-Nur now walks around with a gun.

Since Malam Abdul-Nur returned from the debate with Sheikh in Saudi Arabia, he has been making his people train in the bush as if they were going to war. They travel there at night and they are all made to put on blindfolds so they do not see how to get there. There, they fire weapons and a man from Chad teaches them how to dismantle, assemble and clean guns. If you do not oil guns, Jibril said, they can jam when you are trying to shoot. When I asked if he also had been learning how to use the guns, he went quiet. He asked me to send him recharge cards so he could call me and I sent him a text with two recharge card numbers this morning. I worry for him. He is terrified because already, Malam Abdul-Nur has shot someone in the thigh who was caught trying to leave the premises. 'He even has a little cell, where he keeps people who have committed offences,' Jibril said. He has made me swear not to tell anyone.

It is impressive how no one is late for the screening of the debate. We start at exactly 8 p.m. and the gates to the school are shut. All the men were searched at the gate as they came in. No knives or bottles are allowed in. I got one of the

volunteer guards to set up a table where he would keep and
tag, with masking tape, any knife or bottle that was taken away,
so that the owner could have it back at the end of the film. I
am chewing on my nails and panting like I have been running.
Perhaps I should have watched the debate before showing it.

The film starts playing and Sheikh and Malam Abdul-
Nur are seated, facing each other. Malam Abdul-Nur looks
agitated. You can see that he is grinding his teeth. They each
have ten minutes to speak and five minutes to respond.

Malam Abdul-Nur opens with a long Arabic quotation
from a book by Bakr ibn Abdullah Abu Zayd. He then trans-
lates it into Hausa and explains how Islamic societies were
self-sufficient and pious and progressive. The Europeans,
he explains, needing to conquer Muslim people, sought to
start by conquering their culture through worthless and sin-
ful education. He says that if the Europeans had come with
guns and ships, it might have been easy to fend them off. But
they came with liberal ideas and education to slowly eat at the
root of Islamic civilisation and control. He calls the modern
Islamic universities 'so-called Islamic universities' because
they have adopted Western education. Then he takes a more
direct hit at Sheikh by saying that the basis of the Nigerian
government is kufr because democracy is 'a disgusting, anti-
Islamic, Western invention which seeks to introduce liberal
ideas and kill Islamic values.' He adds that working for the
cause of kufr makes a person a kafir. He emphasises the word
'kafir' and says that it is the obligation of every able Muslim to
forcefully challenge and remove ungodly, infidel rulers. Not
through elections, because elections themselves are part of
a system of kufr, but by force, because Muslims are bound
by submission to the will of Allah.

The crowd is becoming uneasy and offended by the way Malam Abdul-Nur directly calls Sheikh an infidel.

I hear a commotion at the gate and run to see what is going on. When I get there, a policeman is pointing his rifle at one of the volunteer guards and shouting. His colleagues are holding him back.

'What is the matter?' I ask Yushau.

'It is that policeman. One of the boys saw him bring out a small bottle of alcohol from his pocket and told him not to drink it here. That is all.'

I walk over to the shouting policeman.

'Please let us lower our voices,' I say.

'Tell your boys to know how to respect a person wearing a uniform. I am not his playmate.'

'I apologise for how he must have spoken to you. But please help us. We are the ones who want you here. You know this is a religious event and it is against the religion to have alcohol. Please, if you can just wait a bit, until we finish.'

The policeman glowers at the boy who challenged him, then looks at me.

'OK. But tell them not to disrespect me again. Otherwise we will pack up and leave.'

'Done. Thank you, officer.'

I want to speak to the boy directly, but I do not want to make Yushau look bad or weak in front of his boys. I take Yushau aside and explain to him that he needs to make sure he is on top of things and avoid any confrontation with the police. He apologises for not handling the situation well.

When I get back to the debate, Sheikh is asking Malam Abdul-Nur if he had ever been to any of the 'so-called' Islamic universities he is condemning. He asks if Malam Abdul-Nur knows the curriculum of any of them. As Malam Abdul-Nur shakes his head, there are outbursts of 'Allahu Akbar' in the crowd. They are relieved at the comeback.

'To fight an enemy, you must understand an enemy. How do you struggle against those whose elements you know nothing about? Seek knowledge, the Prophet sallallahu alaihi wasallam said. Where are the Muslim schools for our children to attend? Have we built them? I have built one school. But of the millions of Muslim children, how many can go to a Muslim school? Should our people remain ignorant and keep being controlled by the same Western forces? Give me one hadith or Quranic verse that tells you that English itself is haram, even by analogical deduction. If there is, I would like to know. Osama bin Laden, did he go to an Islamic school? Al-Zarqawi, did he go to an Islamic school? Were they not all trained in Western ways? Is that not how they are able to struggle against the West? They learn the tricks of the West well enough to use those tricks against them. You cannot choose deliberate ignorance and claim to be fighting for the cause of Islam. The principle of darura, necessity, means that we use what we have to get what we want.'

'Are you then agreeing with the legitimacy of these systems of kufr over Muslims?' Malam Abdul-Nur interjects.

'Look, I agree with you that the system of the Nigerian government is not a system known to Islam. What Islam knows is khilafa. But just as it is possible to do shirk or bid'a or haram in an Islamic government and be condemned to hellfire, so it is possible to be pious and righteous and uphold halal in an un-Islamic government and receive the reward of aljanna firdaus.'

'So you are saying we fold our hands and do nothing while the West destroys Islam through our infidel government.'

'I am saying, which is more injurious to Muslims, refusing to join the government and refusing to go to school and being sidelined by the government or going to school, pushing for separate classrooms for boys and girls, pushing for girls to wear their hijabs to school, joining government and the police and the army and eventually becoming strong enough to control the government? Look at what Obasanjo did to us—he reduced our numbers in the army and in the police and reduced our influence everywhere. Now you are saying don't go to school, don't be part of government—is that supposed to remedy it or make it worse? When our women and children can't read and write, is this supposed to help them take over Nigeria? Let me ask you a question and I want you to answer. If you got guns and men and tanks and defeated the Nigerian army, what is your plan for ruling this country, especially as there is a whole other half that is not Muslim?'

'Sharia! I will use Sharia! The laws of Allah are self-sufficient.'

'How do you plan to do that all around the country? I am interested to know.'

Malam Abdul-Nur is silent. After a few seconds, Sheikh continues.

'You don't have a plan! You don't even have a plan for defeating the army. All you want is to give into your lust for power and get Muslims killed unnecessarily in the streets. That is what is ignorance—allowing your feelings to guide you instead of thinking of whether this will be good for Muslims or not. This is a dangerous thing you are preaching and if you have the interest of the Muslim ummah at heart, you will stop

it. I will be the happiest if we can replace this government
with an Islamic government. But we must work for it. I am
still extending my invitation to you. Let us continue working
together.'

For a few minutes the film continues playing but neither
of them is speaking. It ends and the crowd begins clapping
wildly and chanting 'Allahu Akbar.' I take a microphone from
the man controlling the projector and tell everyone that we
are grateful that they came and that people should file out
quietly after receiving their drinks and food, which are near
the gates. Men will collect theirs on the right and women on
the left, close to their respective exits.

I check my phone and see that Sheikh has sent me a
text to ask if everything is going fine. I walk into his office
in the school and try to call him. He cuts the call. Then he
calls back.

'What's the story?'

'Wallahi, everything is just perfect, no rowdiness and the
people loved the film.'

'Alhamdulillah! Is there enough for everyone to eat?'

'Insha Allah, Sheikh. I am sure it will go round.'

'Give the policemen thirty thousand before they leave.'

'Sheikh, isn't that too much? There are only sixteen of
them. We can give them twenty thousand so that they can
share at least one thousand per person.'

'OK, if you think so.'

'What of the volunteer guard?'

'You know we don't give them money. Let them have as
much food as they want and let the buses take them wherever they want to go. But we don't want to introduce money.
The police, they are rotten because of this kind of thing. Our

volunteer guard is good because they are not doing it for the money. When they need anything we provide it.'

'OK, Sheikh.'

'Go and sleep when everything is over. We will talk tomorrow. You will tell me what you thought of the film.'

'Allah keep us, Sheikh.'

I see that Jibril has also tried to reach me. I know he said not to call him back but I do anyway. He does not pick up. He sends a text saying he will call me back.

I am tired and sit to rest a bit in the office before going home. I turn on the computer and wipe the dusty keyboard with the tip of my caftan. Sale is a really filthy guy. I don't know how he can work on a table as dirty as this. There is everything, food remnants from the Indomie he orders from the mai shayi near the mosque, oil, dust. I find a rag in the corner of the room and use some water from the plastic kettle to dampen it. I clean the computer monitor, then lift the keyboard to clean the table properly. There is a blank CD beneath the keyboard. I put it aside and continue cleaning.

I am thinking of Microsoft Excel. Sale claims not to know how to use it. I do not know if he really doesn't know or if he just doesn't want to teach me. I lift the keyboard again and pick up the plain CD, open the CD drive and put it in. It is weird how much I like hearing the hum as the drive spins the CD. Windows Media Player comes up and the CD starts playing. The video begins abruptly and I almost jump out of my seat. A man is sitting down, naked, and a naked white woman kneels before him and starts to rub his penis. Then she starts sucking until she takes the whole penis in her mouth. At first it is disgusting how each time she appears to be about to throw up because of how he is pushing his penis deep into her mouth.

A chill is passing through my body. I shut the windows and close the door. My penis is getting harder and harder until I feel like my head is about to burst. I stop the CD, put it back under the keyboard and turn off the computer. Still my head and chest feel like they are about to burst and my penis is still getting harder. It has never been this hard before. Images from the CD flood my mind. All I can see is the woman with the man in her mouth. I loosen my trousers, pull up my caftan, suspend it with my chin and start to stroke. I close my eyes and I see the naked white woman then the naked prostitute behind the tipper garage and then my mind changes the woman's face to Aisha's and she is the one having me in her mouth.

I stroke harder and harder, and then the door just swings open. I freeze in the chair. Sheikh looks at me and steps into the room. My chin releases the caftan and it falls over my penis.

'You know,' Sheikh begins, hiccupping, 'if every man were to be instantly judged for their sins, there would hardly be anyone left standing.'

I feel like the earth beneath me should part and swallow me. It feels like walking through a wedding ceremony with shit on my face.

'I will tell you a story,' he says.

I move in my seat and tighten my trouser slowly beneath my caftan.

'Before people started calling me Sheikh, before anyone knew me in this motor park, maybe even before you were born, I had a wife. Not this one here with me now. Another one. My cousin. Asiya was her name. The one I loved before I knew anything. I loved her before I knew what a woman was.'

The room is suddenly very hot.

'I didn't know what marriage was. My father had arranged my marriage and I took it all for granted. And what did I know? Even when I met Hauwa, who owned the restaurant near my house, what did I know? The first time it happened, Hauwa cried. For days. And she made me swear that I would never tell Asiya. Then she made me agree that I would take her as a second wife. And when I agreed and tried to meet her people, she refused, saying that she had changed her mind and didn't want to be a second wife. Of course I could not do that to Asiya, send her away after less than one year because I wanted to marry another person. And Asiya, who trusted me more than she trusted anyone in the world, didn't suspect anything. She would even beg me sometimes, when she was not feeling strong, to go to Hauwa and buy some food. I had promised Asiya when we were marrying that I would never take a second wife. She said, "No, don't make me that promise. It is sunna for you to take another wife. I cannot let you swear not to do something Allah has made halal for you. It is your right." I said, "Yes, it is, but it is not wajib. I don't have to." So I swore I never would. One day she came home earlier than she should have, you know it is not as if there was GSM then. And she caught us, Hauwa and me, in the living room, without any clothes on.'

Sheikh drags a chair and sits, facing me. I shuffle in my seat, and fold my arms across my lap. He is looking at the ground between us.

'So.' I clear my throat. 'What happened?'

'I left her. Not she. I. Because I had breached a trust. And when I thought how each time I would go out she would suspect that I had been with another woman or always live in fear that I would take another wife, I could not go on like that. She forgave me. We didn't even have to talk about it. She just asked me: "Will you marry her?" and when I said no, all she said was, "Poor woman." We never talked about it again but then each time, I saw that fear in her eyes when I needed to talk to her about something or when I returned home. She would stare deep into my eyes as if she was waiting for me to say I was going to bring another woman home. I could not just keep on paying for that moment and being with someone who would never trust me again. So I left her. And, you know, my friends, they insulted me—they said I was taking my wife too seriously. And they were right. I did take her seriously. She was not just my cousin. She was the best friend I had.'

It feels like we are both standing naked in this room and I do not know which is worse—his nakedness, or mine. I look up at him and he looks up too.

'Are you waiting for me to say something? That is the end of my story.'

He gets up and walks to the door.

'Were you wondering what the moral of the story was?' he asks, turning around.

'Yes, Sheikh,' I reply.

'There is no moral. I just felt like telling you a story.'

FOCAL

1. Principal: main and most important.

In my heart, Aisha is FOCAL.

SECT

1. a religious group that is connected to a larger group but that has beliefs that differ greatly from those of the main group.
2. a religious group that is a smaller part of a larger group and whose members all share similar beliefs.

When I am hearing Sheikh preaching or hearing news on radio or reading Sheikh books, I am thinking of the way people are fighting Muslim people in all the world and I am thinking that if all Muslim people are not fighting each other then maybe other kafir people will not have the power over us. Every time I am looking at the CD where Malam and Sheikh are not agreeing, I am wishing that everything is in the Quran, all the questions people are fighting about, so that people will not be fighting over what is correct and what is not correct. Allah forgive me. Because maybe if everything was there Sheikh and Malam will not be fighting. But there are people that even if every thing is in the Quran, they will still bring their own thinking into it to cause fighting. Maybe some people just like to fight. I don't understand. Allah forgive me.

Tolls

Politics is very time consuming. These days Sheikh hardly shows up at the mosque: I haven't seen him in three days. I go with him to a lot of meetings and the last one went from 9 a.m. until 6 p.m. I chew lots of kola to stop myself from falling asleep. Kola makes my stomach swell and gives me gas, but gas is better than dozing off when I have to take notes. Sheikh doesn't chew kola at all. I wonder how he stays awake.

'You are a lazy man,' Sheikh often jokes when I start to chew.

No one, not even Alhaji Usman, knows who will contest for the governorship. The deputy governor has been unclear about this and it frustrates Alhaji Usman. He thinks the deputy governor is deliberately not saying anything. The governor has had his two terms. He is not interested in being a senator and has refused to endorse any candidate ahead of the Big Party primaries. But there are rumours everywhere and no one is sure whether he is giving money to the deputy governor or to Alhaji Usman or both of them. Alhaji Usman has refused to print any posters until the deputy governor says what office he is interested in.

Alhaji Usman has doubled the amount of food he gives on Fridays and added bars of soap to the distribution. Soap has become popular especially after the cholera outbreak, when there were daily jingles on the radio about keeping clean and washing often. People are calling the soap Sabulun Usman. At first Alhaji Usman angered all the shop sellers whose sales were affected by all the free soap that suddenly flooded the town. When the market association sent a delegation to meet him, he apologised, gave them money and arranged to buy the soap directly from them. So now, if you buy things from any of the shops in the market, you will get a free bar of washing and bathing soap. Everyone is happy with this arrangement.

The deputy governor gives cash to people during rallies. His posters, which simply have his face and the words 'Sai Ka Yi,' do not say anything about what office he wants.

Jibril is scaring me with these texts he sends from different numbers. Malam Abdul-Nur made them all give up their phones when they moved to his new farm in a remote village I have never heard of.

'Shooting makes me feel both scared and as if someone is shocking my body with electricity. Shooting makes me feel like I have drunk something to make me high.'

I have never fired a gun but I know the feeling he is talking about. It is the same way I felt when we were burning things. The only high better than that is the high of wee-wee. Everything becomes slightly blurry and it feels like I am standing on a moving platform above everyone around me. In that moment I feel like no one is capable of doing anything to me. But it is the feeling afterwards that makes me glad I don't get high anymore. Like how I felt after all that burning in Bayan Layi. It felt like someone had tied my intestines in tight knots and the whole world was crashing on my head. And that horrible feeling lasts longer than being high.

There are tents everywhere, he says, and the farm itself is like a small village. Because Malam Abdul-Nur has his boys patrolling the whole village at night and has dug two wells, he forces the village head to pay him a weekly tax. The Mujahideen do not use cars or phones. I am happy he has taken his weird movement far away from us. It is the people in that village I feel sorry for.

After the evening prayers Sheikh walks into my office and sits down.

'What is the problem?' he begins. 'I have given you enough time I believe and you still act as if what I told you is not important. It is sunna to marry. You do not have to wait until you find the best woman. You do not even have to like her. Find a good girl and we will conduct the marriage.'

'I found a girl,' I say, 'but it seems she does not like me.'

'Why do you think so?'

'Because I used to talk to her and even call her on the phone, but now she doesn't take my calls.'

'You are smart in the things of religion but it seems you need to be tutored in the ways of life. When a woman does not like you, then she will not care about you at all. She will not bother to hide herself from you. But when a woman takes the time to hide from you and doesn't take your phone calls then she is playing a game. This is how our women are.'

'Then what do I do?'

'She needs to know you are not one of these useless men around town and that you are serious. Show her you are serious. Just tell her you are going to talk to her father and see what she says. How old is she?'

'I didn't ask.'

'What do you mean you didn't ask? I am not going to do your background work for you. Find out all these details, how old she is, who her father is, if she has ever been married before and then let me know. I can't believe I have to tell you all this.'

'OK, Sheikh.'

'What of Jibril, do you hear from him at all?'

'Only to tell me that he is OK. They have been stopped from using phones.'

'Madman. Abdul-Nur is mad. He is doing this because I floored him in the debate. He is trying to prove to me that he can run an Islamic state. But he will kill all those people. If Jibril has any sense, he will find his way out of there before his brother leads them all to destruction. I even hear that in the village where he is, people are leaving because they are afraid of him. In just a short while he has taken over everything and terrorises everyone including the village head. Allah forbid! If there is any one mistake I made, it is Abdul-Nur. Now I can't even look Alhaji Usman in the eye because he will say he told me. Everyone told me but I thought I had him under control. A Yoruba man is a Yoruba man. No matter how Muslim they become. They stab you in the back. That is how they are. Hypocrites.'

Sheikh is angrier than I have ever seen him. There are tears in his eyes as he speaks. This will be the wrong time to tell him about Aisha. Usually I am sure how he will react to

something—I think I know him that well. This time I have
no idea if he will give me a big handshake or a big slap. In my
head I want to agree about Yoruba people because everyone
says it and you can always find examples, but then I remember
that Jibril is Yoruba too. He has never stabbed me in the back.

We have lost one of our major funders in Saudi Arabia. I did not know of this funder until I started handling
our second bank account. There was money coming from
the Maliki Foundation, which stopped a few months before
Malam Abdul-Nur came back. The Foundation hosted Malam
Abdul-Nur when he first got to Saudi Arabia. They gave him
everything he needed because he was from Sheikh. When
Sheikh called to ask if there was a problem, they told him they
would send him an email. Two weeks after, they emailed to
say that they had suspended the project under which we were
receiving assistance. We do not know what happened when
Malam Abdul-Nur was there or what he told them about us
but Sheikh has found out that they are the ones who gave
him money to buy and build up his farm. Sheikh says he will
travel with the next hajj and try to have a meeting with them.
He has added my name to the next hajj list too. Now I need to
go and get a passport from the Immigration office in Sokoto.

I discovered something else while handling that account.
When he announces a donation, Alhaji Usman only gives us
a third of what he announces. The money comes through his
company, which makes a payment to us by cheque or by bank
transfer. I then withdraw two-thirds of the amount and give
it back to him in cash. Then we multiply all our expenses by
three. So even though what we spent on the building of the
school was eighteen million, our papers read fifty-four million.
I do not know how to feel about this.

*　*　*

When I leave the house to go to the mosque, everyone is huddled in groups listening to the radio. People are sad and shaking their heads and talking in hushed tones. In the mosque Malam Yunusa is speaking with Malam Abduljalal and a few other men.

'Salamu alaikum,' I say to them on my way into the office.

'Wa alaikum wassalam,' they chorus.

'You have heard what happened?' Malam Yunusa asks.

'No, what happened?'

'The governor has died ai.'

'Inna lillahi wa inna ilaihi raji'un,' I sigh; 'how did he die?'

'An aircraft crash. He went down south with others in a helicopter to attend a wedding. He died together with the former inspector general of police, who was from Sokoto.'

Sheikh calls to say he will not be around all evening. He and Alhaji Usman are going to Government House to see the deputy governor. Life is funny and one never knows why Allah destines these things to occur. What causes mourning in one house causes rejoicing in another; one family cries while another gives thanks to Allah. The deputy governor may mourn but there is no way his family will not rejoice at his sudden elevation. And at least Alhaji Usman now knows that the Senate seat is free for him to contest.

I call Aisha. She does not pick up. Women can be very annoying. Sometimes they are very nice and they make you stay up all night thinking about them, unable to breathe because you feel your heart wanting to jump out of your chest. Other times they act as if the world is theirs to take, as if men were made to fulfil their every need.

'What is it?' she texts me.

I dial her number again. Every ring feels like hot stones pushed through my ear.

'Yes?' she says.

'Salamu alaikum,' I reply.

'Amin alaikum wassalam.'

'I'm sorry, but I just wanted to find out if you got the wrapper I sent you.'

'Yes I got your message loud and clear because all I have are green hijabs ko? And you need to save me from embarrassment because I need clothes. Yes, mister, I got your message. And I might have returned it if I did not need a rag so urgently.'

'May Allah calm your temper, Aisha, I did not mean to insult you. Forgive me if I have acted foolishly.'

She goes silent for a few seconds and then says in a less impatient voice, 'What do you want?'

'I want to ask your father,' I say.

'Ask him what?'

'I'm not joking around. I want to marry you, Aisha.'

The line goes dead. I know she has dropped the call but I call back. It rings for a while before she picks up.

'Aisha, did you hear what I said earlier?' I ask.

'Yes,' she mumbles.

'Do you have anything to say then?'

'First,' she says, almost whispering, 'I don't know you like that. And second, this is not how to tell someone you want to marry her. Why do you want to marry me? Are you not too young to marry even?'

'First,' I reply, 'one does not get to know a person in one day. Even when one has been with someone for many years one still learns new things. And to your second question, I like you, Aisha. I like you and I think you are a decent, hardworking girl. I like you, Aisha.'

'So if you like me, is that not what you should have said first? How do you tell a person you want to marry them first, and then after, that you like them? Me, I do not understand this. A man woos a woman. It is not like I do not have options. How do I know that you are serious?'

'Forgive me Aisha that I have gotten the other things wrong but I thought to go straight to the point since you hardly ever take my calls. And if you let me, I will woo you.'

She is silent for a while. 'My mother needs me, I have to go,' she says.

'So, will you pick up the next time I call?'

'I don't know. Won't you have to try to find out?'

'That is true,' I say.

My heart is beating against my chest like a dog trying to get out of its cage. I feel like reaching into my chest and opening the cage. The phone rings again and without looking I pick up and say: 'Aisha.'

'It's Jibril,' the voice whispers back.

'Oh, Jibril. What's up?'

'I am afraid,' he says.

'What has happened now?'

'He has gone crazy!'

'Has she told him?'

'Yes and he thinks it is his but that is not the issue. He chopped off someone's hand today.'

'What? What!'

'Someone said he stole some raw meat after they slaughtered a cow.'

'And nobody said anything?'

'He made everybody watch, and I was in front. He used the butcher's axe. I've never seen so much blood in my life. He has gone crazy!'

'When did this happen?'

'Early this morning. The boy died about an hour ago. The bleeding refused to stop. They are digging the grave on the edge of the farm.'

'Jibril, you have to run away.'

'I can't. Where will I run to? Anyway, it is not that I can't run away, but I need her to come with me. I can't leave her there with my child. That is my plan. To leave with her.'

'Jibril! This is not the time to be thinking of all this. Would you feel better if you were dead? If you die she will continue life like she never met you before. And your child will never know you.'

'I know she will come with me. I just need to have a good plan to escape, that's all.'

'Jibril! Don't go and put yourself into more trouble fa!'

'Look, I have to go. I will call you again tomorrow.'

When Alhaji Usman walks in to the mosque with Sheikh, people crowd around them, hoping to hear news about their visit to the deputy governor. As Sheikh and Alhaji Usman chat with the other trustees, I try to make sure that the sound system is working properly.

'What are you doing there?' Sheikh calls out to me.

'Checking to make sure everything is OK.'

'Let one of the other boys do that.'

I walk over to where they are all standing.

'Ahmad,' Alhaji Usman says, stretching out his hand. I receive his with both of mine.

'They will swear him in after the burial tomorrow,' Sheikh says to Malam Yunusa, continuing the conversation they were having before I came.

'So, what has been happening?' Sheikh says, turning to me.

'Nothing,' I say.

After a bit of silence I add, 'Jibril called again today.'

'What are they up to now?' Sheikh asks.

'Who is Jibril?' Alhaji Usman asks.

'Oh, that is Abdul-Nur's younger brother. He said they killed someone today,' I continue. 'Someone they said was a thief.'

'What did he steal?' Malam Abduljalal asks.

'They said meat.'

'Meat?' Alhaji Usman exclaims.

'They chopped off the boy's hand and he bled to death.'

'We should have chopped off the infidel's hands. A thief like him, chopping off people's hands for stealing meat?' Malam Yunusa seems more upset than all of them.

'And where is the village head in all of this?' Alhaji Usman asks.

'Ah,' Sheikh exclaims, 'I hear the village head is so scared of him that he is as good as one of his members.'

'In fact, I hear they had a clash with the police only a few days ago,' Malam Yunusa says. 'A policeman tried to arrest one of their members, and they gave the policeman the beating of his life. If he hadn't run away they would have killed him.'

'Honestly, I will talk to His Excellency about this,' Alhaji Usman says. 'How can some Yoruba convert come here and be doing all of this? We will send him back to whatever bush he came from. Sheikh please remind me about this.'

Every time Sheikh preaches after prayers I think that if the only favour Allah would grant me is to preach like this, then I need no more favours. The mosque is full and there is no one making side talk as Sheikh speaks about the death of the governor, the cluelessness of the federal government and why we need to support and vote for a Muslim president in the next elections. Then he starts talking about the Mujahideen.

'Some of the worst enemies of Islam are the ones who deceive innocent people into thinking they are Muslims. Somebody who has no understanding of Islam and its precepts will go around calling himself a Mujahideen. Islam does not put people in bondage like they are doing, or in fear. These are the people who are our greatest enemies, the traitors from within. You sit on a farm with ignorant people around you and alone pass fatwas according to your whims. How is that sharia? How is that Islam? I tell you, even if they do not get their punishment now, Allah will ask them on the last day.'

I stare at him as he speaks, noticing the bags under his eyes and how his right hand has started to tremble. Many days he preaches with passion but some days with anger. Like today. I can tell when he is angry from the froth at the side of his mouth and the pursing of his lips. He is angry about Abdul-Nur and about losing the Saudi grant and about the policemen at the checkpoints who harass people.

I wait until all the people who want to speak to Sheikh have left before telling him what is on my mind. This isn't the best time, but I can't keep this any longer.

'About the marriage issue, Sheikh . . .'

'Yes?'

'Forgive me, I should have told you earlier. I spoke to the girl again.'

'OK, and?'

'I should have told you it was . . .'

'Yes? Should I beg before you say who it is? Who is her father?'

'Actually, it is Aisha.'

'Which Aisha?'

'Your Aisha.'

I can see that Sheikh is trying hard not to show that he is uncomfortable about this. He opens his mouth several times to say something but nothing comes out.

'Why didn't you say this before?' Sheikh says finally. 'What was all the secrecy about?'

'I'm sorry, Sheikh. I did not know how you would react.'

'I think we should talk about this tomorrow. I've had a very long day,' Sheikh says, and walks away.

I am upset. If I am good enough to handle his money and our movement then I should be good enough to take care of Aisha. Except if, astaghfirullah, all the grand things he says about me in my presence and when I am not there are all lies. But then, perhaps a daughter is not the same thing as a bank account.

I dial Aisha's number.

'You didn't even let it ring,' I say.

'No, I was already fiddling with the phone when your call came in.'

'So I hope your day has gone well?'

'Alhamdulillah, everything went well.'

'Won't you ask me how mine was?'

'Well, if you want me to know how your day was, I am sure you will tell me.'

'OK, my day was fine. I might go with your father to attend the governor's funeral early in the morning. They have found his corpse and are bringing it this night.'

'May Allah forgive him.'

'Amen. So, I spoke to your father.'

'What did you tell him?'

'Just that I am interested and I have started talking to you.'

'What did he say?'

'He hasn't said anything yet. He was so tired from going around today and he said we will talk in the morning.'

'And so am I. I have a lot of work to do in the morning.'

'Oh, I am sorry for calling so late. Is it too late?'

'Yes.'

'OK, I will try to call earlier. Rest well.'

'Umm, sorry . . . about the wrapper you sent—I was only joking earlier. I sent it to the tailor this afternoon.'

'Women ko!' I laugh.

'Men ko!' she laughs.

I am staring at my plaster ceiling, thinking of my Umma. Aisha makes me think of her a lot. Who knows what Umma would have said, if she would have liked Aisha.

My mother's voice is leaving me. Her face is clear in my head, her deep eyes, her smile, her slender, beautiful fingers. I close my eyes to bring up her voice, to make her speak in my ear, in my head, but all I see is her smile. Will I lose this too? Her face in my head? Will it all pass and leave behind a shadow where there was once Umma?

*   *   *

Jibril's call wakes me up in the middle of the night.

'She refused to come with me,' he says, his voice breaking. 'She just said she would rather stay.'

'I am sorry, Jibril.'

'I will leave as soon as he falls asleep. He doesn't sleep until two in the morning.'

'Where will you go?'

'If I go back to Ilorin, he will know where to find me. There is nowhere I can hide there.'

'Jibril, honestly you should have left since. I don't know why you are still there.'

'I know. I don't know why I was foolish enough to think that she wanted me. Imagine, he treats her like an animal, yet she chooses him.'

'Just forget about her. You will find another woman, believe me. A better woman.'

'I don't want a better woman. I want her and I want my child!'

'OK, I hear you. The issue now is what do you do? You can always go back for your child.'

'I know a guy in Makurdi. My friend. He trades in second-hand shoes from Cotonou. I will try to go there. Maybe I can even get to Cotonou. I have to go now.'

'Just take care, and call me when you are settled. Allah guide you safely.'

I am falling asleep at the tap as we all perform ablution. The men around me, who are washing their arms and feet and faces, are talking about the helicopter crash and how they think the president may be behind the crash. Someone reminds the rest of them that the former Inspector General, who was travelling with the governor, had been exposing the secrets of this government. I am not interested in any of this. All I am hoping for is that this sleep does not embarrass me when I will have to talk to Sheikh later. As I wash my face, my eyes hurt from staring at the ceiling all night.

Singing the call to prayer is like a drug, it cures everything for five minutes. Air fills my chest and on its way out forms the words:

Allahu Akbar
Allahu Akbar . . .

My body is transported with those words to a wide dark expanse of nothingness. I am alive. After the call I am as alert as one who has slept all night. Sheikh has not told me how early he will leave for the governor's burial, or if I will go with him. He hasn't said anything and I don't want to ask. I will wait until he raises the issue of Aisha and if he doesn't by the end of the day, I will ask tomorrow.

The sound of motorcycles ridden roughly is drowning out Sheikh's voice as he begins speaking just after the prayer. As the noise increases, I step out to see what is happening. Sometimes it seems to me like a motorcycle is an evil jinn, which, once given to a normal human being, drives him crazy. There are boys in the motor park who are even too shy to speak in public, but on their motorcycles they act like they own the world.

I walk out and see men in police uniforms getting off the motorcycles and heading towards the mosque. I open my mouth to ask what is going on, when they start firing. My head tells me to run into the mosque but my body jumps the short fence and runs into the darkness behind the trees where broken down buses are parked. I lie flat on the ground and hear the men screaming and firing. I get up slowly and peep from behind one of the buses. The policemen are shooting at people trying to run out of the mosque through the doors and the windows. One by one they enter the building. I make to scale the fence, to go and save Sheikh. I stop. His words come to me crisp and clear:

> . . . the president and vice president never travel together in the same plane . . .
>
> . . . someone has to take over in case something happens to one person . . .

I am fighting with myself, holding myself down. After a couple of minutes there is silence. They drag Sheikh out and make him kneel by the taps. They take off his turban. One of the men is taking photos with a small camera. I cannot hear what they are telling him as they slap him across the cheek. They tie his hands behind his back and lay him on the ground. Then one of the men brings out a short knife. He steps on Sheikh's head then rolls him over to make him lie on his belly. The man steps on Sheikh's back and pulls his hair to expose his throat. As two others pin Sheikh down, the man begins to cut.

Running

Malam Yunusa's trembling hand makes shadows dance on the wall as he walks to hang the lantern on a nail. In the empty room behind the mosque, six of us stand around the body: Alhaji Usman, the trustees, Sheikh's old uncle Abdulrahman and I. They all agree that being closest to Sheikh, I should do the washing. There is no electricity but Abdulrahman prefers that we use lanterns instead of a generator so that we do not attract attention.

'Have you ever washed before?' Malam Hamza asks.

'No, but I have been present at two washings.'

'Good, so do you know what to do?'

'Yes, I do.'

I lay three pieces of white cotton cloth on the second, empty table, one on top of the other, and drag the buckets of water close to the first table, where the body lies. Abdulrahman hangs smaller strips of cloth on his shoulder, ready to hand them to me.

I cover the genitals with one strip of cloth and wind another strip around my right hand.

'Bismillahi,' I begin, pouring water over the body. Starting from the stump of the neck, I scrub off the bloodstains gently and make my way to the right shoulder. As I wash I change the strips wrapped around my hand, dumping the old ones in a basket.

If only it was not wrong to make comments on the body while washing I would curse the people who mutilated Sheikh so. I use my right shoulder to wipe a tear that has just dropped from my eyes. After washing the left side of the body, I put my right hand beneath the cloth covering the genitals and wash. Alhaji Usman helps me pour the water. There is still some blood after the third wash, so I wash two more times. For the last round, I add camphor to the water. Alhaji Usman hands me a large towel. I dry the body and dump the towel in the basket. They all help to lift Sheikh onto the table with the three white cloths. After this my mind deserts me and I am not in control of my hands as we shroud the body and take it into the bus outside.

Four men have already been sent to dig the grave. Alhaji Usman and Malam Abduljalal have been making calls to a few family heads in our movement so that they can attend the funeral which is in one hour.

'We do not want all the young men to gather and start a riot,' Alhaji Usman says. Everyone else agrees.

Throughout the funeral I am floating. I am suspended in water and the words are bubbles in my ears. Everyone is a fish swimming past me. I do not know how my legs carry me to the burial ground and from there to Alhaji Usman's house. I do not know how my hands perform the ablution in the small mosque in front of Alhaji Usman's house when dawn arrives, how my knees take me to the ground and bring me back up during the prayer, how I finally end up in Sheikh's house, early in the morning, together with hundreds of mourners.

The fresh wailing of the women behind the house pulls me out of my trance. I listen for Aisha's voice. Even though Alhaji Usman begged everyone not to mention the fact that Sheikh's head was taken away, the women have heard somehow.

Sheikh's family is called into the large living room when the governor arrives. Soldiers and men in plain clothes carrying huge black guns fill up the room, glowering at everyone seated. The governor says a short prayer and gives a rambling speech about how this attack was part of an effort to throw the state and his regime into anarchy and how his government will not stand by and watch while people are made to live in fear.

'As I live and as Allah gives me strength, we will get them,' he says to Sheikh's wife, whose eyes are red and swollen.

'This is not the only one. They attacked three police stations last night and this morning and killed several people. That is where they got the police uniforms. They are enemies of our people and enemies of Islam and I tell you, insha Allah, we will get them.'

He gives Sheikh's wife six hundred thousand naira to buy 'water for the guests' and makes a pledge of one million naira to the family. The money will be delivered to them within the week, he says.

Aisha is looking away, distant. She is not crying and her eyes are not red. She is blinking slowly like one who is drowsy. Her face is blank, revealing nothing. She is hunched and her hands are folded across her stomach. I notice for the first time that she has big breasts. Allah forgive me, I do not know why this is coming to my mind at this time.

I am lying down at home around midday when Alhaji Usman calls to tell me about Abdul-Nur.

'They have caught him. Go to Yunusa's house and tell him. I can't reach any of them by phone.'

Alhaji Usman is out of breath.

'OK, Alhaji. But who caught him?'

'The soldiers. They have taken him to police headquarters to hand him over to the police. They arrested him as he was trying to leave Sokoto.'

'Alhamdulillah.'

'They need to know because the police may invite them for questioning.'

'OK, I will go there immediately.'

In Malam Yunusa's house, all the trustees are already gathered.

'We just heard,' Malam Abduljalal says when I start to recount what Alhaji Usman told me.

They tell me more details. He was caught travelling in a truck, with bundles of crisp dollar notes, trying to go across the border. There were machine guns in the trunk. He cried like a little child as they dragged him away.

'You cannot fight Allah. Hypocrite infidel! How did he think he was going to win? He wanted us to think it was the police so that our boys would attack the police and get killed. I wish they would give him to us so we can cut him to pieces while he is still alive.'

Malam Hamza is frothing at the mouth, trembling, breathing very hard. The rest of them are quiet, rolling their prayer beads.

'We will leave the mosque and school closed,' Malam Abduljalal says, 'we don't want our boys to gather and become agitated. Especially now that, Alhamdulillah, it seems we will have respite with the arrest of Abdul-Nur.'

'I agree,' Malam Yunusa says, 'at least for now.'

It is time for isha and we pray together.

After the prayer I ask if they need me to get them anything.

'Koko. Me, I feel like koko and kosai. Does anyone want some?' They all want what Malam Yunusa wants.

I walk a few streets away, to where Saudatu fries kosai.

'Young man, how is the city heat?' she says without looking up from the large frying pan.

I hate being called young man, especially by a woman.

'The city is indeed hot,' I say, hiding my irritation, 'what can one do but give thanks to Allah.'

'How is the mourning?'

'Alhamdulillah.'

'I hear they caught the Mujahideen leader today. They say he abandoned his people and tried to run away.'

'How did you hear that?'

'Haba young man, is there anything that Saudatu does not know? That I am frying kosai on a street corner does not make me stupid.'

'Yes, I heard the same thing.'

'I don't know why people would not learn. Someone asks you to die for him, yet when it comes to it, he himself is afraid of death.'

I have no idea where she gets her stories from. She reminds me of a woman who was notorious for gossiping in Dogon Icce. My Umma would say of her: 'If you are shitting in the bush and you see her walking by, sit on it.'

'Is that not how they told us that, during the Civil War, the same man who was pushing the Nyamirai to attack Nigeria jumped on a plane and ran away when he saw that his people were defeated? People never learn. Allah knows why he made me barren, because, wallahi, I would strangle any child of mine that chooses to join such a group. I would poison him and, wallahi, I would sleep well after that.'

I smile and take the kosai from her. 'I will come back for the koko.'

'No, let this little girl follow you with it.' She hands the girl a big plastic bowl wrapped in a black polythene bag. 'Maryam, if you like, act like a bastard and don't come back here quickly,' Saudatu says as we walk away.

In the morning the rumours begin. They say Malam Abdul-Nur is no longer at police headquarters in Sokoto. I keep telling people it is a lie and that Alhaji Usman, a friend to the governor, has told me so. It is scary how rumours travel and how the story changes as it travels. Everywhere people are gathered in groups, talking loud and angry. Some boys are holding sticks. I call Alhaji Usman. He tells me he will call me right back.

After an hour, I call Malam Yunusa.

'We have to be careful with this information because we do not know what is going on or who called from Abuja to secure his release.'

'Why would anyone release him,' I protest.

'Well, apparently someone doesn't want him to talk. There is someone involved at a very high level.'

'What do we tell people? Because I have been telling everyone that it is a lie.'

'This old man has no answers. But let's wait until we have more information. If people become violent because of this, it is nobody's fault but the police and the government. They brought it on themselves.'

'Have you spoken to Alhaji Usman?'

'No. I think he is busy.'

Outside the mosque, boys are gathering and piling old tyres. Everyone has a stick or machete. The police have disappeared from the streets. People begin to scream and burn the tyres and write on walls with charcoal: 'We don't want Mujahideen.'

A group of boys drag a man to where the tyres are burning. A crowd quickly gathers. They beat him, first with whips, then with sticks. I make my way to the middle but cannot recognise his face because of all the blood. I will not stand by while they do this. I intervene.

'How do you know he is a Mujahideen?' I ask.

'Because he admitted it. He was trying to recruit a young boy on our street.'

'Where is the young boy?'

They push forward a frowning little boy.

'What did he say to you?' I ask the boy.

'He said I should follow him and that if I fight for Islam they will take care of me and my family. He gave me money.'

The man is barely able to sit up. Someone hits him with a stick on the shoulders.

'Because of Allah, show mercy,' he cries, 'I am a Muja-hideen but I swear to you I repent from this day. I can show you where the others are.'

'Tell us who the others are!' the crowd cries.

He mumbles some names. I think of Sheikh's headless body and I step back from the crowd.

'Kill him,' people are beginning to shout.

They tie a rope around his neck and suspend him from a mango tree nearby. And pelt him with stones.

In just a few hours tyres are burning everywhere and at least two more Mujahideen have been killed. Malam Abdul-Nur's former house, now empty, has been set ablaze together with the houses of the men who were killed. Alhaji Usman still hasn't called back. When I try to call again his phone is switched off. There are large numbers of people chanting, 'No more Mujahideen' in the streets. Cars are being stopped and searched. Drivers who are stubborn or who ask too many questions are beaten.

I am floating again.

The streets begin to empty at night when the army trucks begin to arrive. On the radio, the governor declares a dusk-till-dawn curfew in the state and asks everyone to stay indoors or face arrest. The soldiers begin to occupy all the abandoned police checkpoints. I leave the mosque area from where I have been tracking events and head home.

I want to call Aisha. But what do I say to a girl whose father has just been beheaded?

Outside Sheikh's house, where the trustees and I are saying prayers to mark the third day of mourning, a crowd has gathered. We step out and Malam Yunusa asks Malam Abduljalal to address the agitated crowd. Malam Hamza begs to take his leave because he is weak and his bones hurt from arthritis. I bring out two benches and turn them into a makeshift stage for Malam Abduljalal. Alhaji Usman is on my right, his arms folded across his chest. Malam Yunusa is looking in my eyes. He leans in to whisper.

'You have to speak to the crowd next. I don't want to see tears. This is not the time for it, this is not the place for it.'

I snuffle a few times and heave deeply. The chatter among people is getting louder and I can barely hear Malam Abduljalal speaking.

'Are you OK?' Malam Yunusa asks. I nod.

In the distance, I see four soldiers approaching. When they get behind the crowd, they stop. Malam Yunusa looks at them, looks at me and mutters, 'Bastard sons of goats.' I smile. I have never heard him curse before and it sounds really funny coming from him. At some point Malam Abduljalal goes quiet like he has forgotten what he wants to say. Malam Yunusa tugs at his caftan then nudges me to go up. When I climb the benches the whispering stops. I scream, 'Allahu Akbar!' The response of the crowd is better than the first time I smoked wee-wee. It is hard to describe it, the thunderous response following the silence of an eager crowd, thousands of eyes gazing upon me, hundreds of palms waving in the air holding on to your words, fired up. And in that moment, astaghfirullah, you feel like a prophet. I am not listening to myself, I am not forming the words that are leaping out of my mouth into the air and into the ears of the hundreds of people here. A force is driving me that I do not know, but, wallahi, I love it. I love it even though the soldiers look menacing and have their fingers on their triggers, ready to shoot. I can see fear in their eyes. I love that even though they are coming closer, no one seems to care. The soldiers go round on the right side of the crowd and approach where we are standing. Alhaji Usman steps away from us to speak to them. They are arguing and pointing at me. I keep on speaking. Alhaji Usman leaves them and whispers to Malam Yunusa. Malam Yunusa in turn whispers into my ear.

'They want the crowd to disperse; they say all public gathering and preaching is prohibited. At this point I don't care what you do as long as the people are with you. Do you want to disperse the crowd or do you want to go on?'

I think a bit about the soldiers going crazy and hurting people, but with the large and angry crowd, these four men will have no choice but to turn away. I smile at him and continue speaking.

Alhaji Usman walks away. Malam Abduljalal follows him.

Malam Yunusa moves closer to me. Soldiers begin to shout at people, asking them to leave and go home. They are hitting and pushing people. When one of them fires a shot in the air, people scream and start to throw stones at them. The soldiers shoot into the crowd. Some run away but most people stand their ground, pelting the soldiers with even bigger stones. I get down from the benches and pick up a stone. The crowd is closing in on them. The soldiers start to back away and then begin to run, shooting as they do. The crowd pursues. A large stone gets one of the soldiers in the neck. He trips and falls. As we all surge forward to where the soldier has fallen, I turn around to look for Malam Yunusa. He is there, a few feet behind me, lying motionless in the dust beside one of the boys of the volunteer guard. Tears well up in my eyes as I drag his body and lean it against a wall. By the time I reach where the soldier is lying, the crowd has torn off his uniform and smashed his head with stones and sticks. A human body without a face does not look like a human being.

I am back in my room, folding a few clothes into my bag, wondering if Sheikh would have listened to the soldiers and dispersed the crowd or continued speaking, if I have made Sheikh proud or disappointed him. I have never felt the ground tremble the way it does now under the armoured tanks that roll onto the street. The sound of the guns they are shooting now are different from the ones the soldiers who came to disperse the crowd were shooting. I will not wait until the soldiers start destroying the town and killing people.

I cannot reach my brothers on the phone. I dial Aisha's number.

'I am sorry I haven't called you until now. I didn't know what to say.'

'It's OK,' she whispers.

'How do you feel?'

'I'm fine.'

'Are you at home?'

'We just got to Kaduna. I'm sorry I didn't tell you. It all happened so quickly.'

'Why are you whispering?'

'Because there are people all around me.'

'How long will you be there?'

'Call me later please. My mum is here. There are people all around.'

'I have to travel too. The whole place is hot now. There is a riot. I will call you when I get to Dogon Icce.'

'May Allah forbid mishaps on the road.'

I am not sure if she heard me say there is a riot.

As I approach the motor park, I realise I have to fight for a bus. I put the strap of my bag across my chest and grip it as I run. The fare has doubled. I don't care. I just need to get out of this place. Everyone in the bus complains, some raining curses on the driver for taking advantage of a desperate situation.

'Whoever doesn't want it can get out of my bus.'

We take dirt roads through residential areas. There is dust everywhere. The route is longer but the driver says it will avoid the checkpoints. He just returned from Dogon Icce, so he should know.

Everyone is telling him to stop as he tries to cross an open gutter. He tells us to shut up and that he is in charge, before running right into it and getting stuck. No one wants to help him push the bus but no one wants to remain here either. In the end we have to lift the bus and put stones and wooden planks beneath the two front tires before he is able to drive out of the gutter. Everyone is running away, but after defying the soldiers only this morning, I feel like a coward in this bus. Like a rat scampering through dirt roads.

If Jibril was able to make it out, he must be in Makurdi by now.

Towards the end of the last dirt road that leads onto one of the main tarred roads, the driver tells everyone to hold on. He wants to speed right into the road just in case there are any soldiers around the corner. He screeches onto the tarred road. In the distance there is a truck coming our way. As we come closer we realise it is an army truck. The driver slows down and tries to make a U-turn. The truck honks and the soldiers start shooting and screaming. People in the bus start screaming at the driver, telling him to stop. As soon as the driver parks on the side of the road, the two men in the front seats get out and begin to run. The truck pulls over behind us and several soldiers jump out, firing shots in the air. As we all get down from the bus with our hands in the air, four soldiers emerge from the dirt road with the two men who just ran away.

'You are the people who kill soldiers abi?' one of the soldiers shouts at the two men. One of the men spits on the soldiers. A soldier from the truck kicks them both to the floor and shoots them in the chest and in the head. They order us to lie flat on the hot asphalt and they tie our hands behind our backs with wire.

Counting Days

Day One

At first some things seem like a joke. I hear stories of things happening to others, I hear the words—people disappearing, people's hands getting chopped off, people getting beaten and people dying. The words produce pictures in my mind but it is nothing compared with experiencing it. When Sheikh told me about being arrested and being detained for eight weeks for involvement in a riot where a boy in his school was killed, it was just a story. Until I woke up with my hands sore from being bound tightly behind my back, none of it was real.

I am lying in a room with people pissing on themselves and throwing up and crying. One man has been lying still since they threw him in. A man I recognise from the motor park is bleeding from his right ear and falling in and out of consciousness. They must at least let us relieve ourselves or pray at some point. None of this makes any sense. I cannot tell where we are because we were blindfolded with rags on the way here.

The sun is high and I can see the steam rising from people's bodies. My throat is dry and it is painful to swallow saliva. My back itches terribly. I make my way to a wall and rub my back against it.

I can no longer hold back the urge to pee. Slowly I let the warm fluid trickle down my legs making the fabric stick to my skin. The man in front of me doesn't even shift his feet as the urine reaches him. Everyone is too traumatised to care about urine on the floor.

I have failed Sheikh and let the movement down. I have let my brothers down. I grit my teeth and struggle to free my hands until I have no energy left. My hands burn. My eyes burn. My heart burns.

At night the soldiers take turns banging the metal doors with sticks for nearly an hour. At first my head pounds but after a while I don't hear the sounds anymore.

Day Two

People are being taken out every few hours in groups of three.

'The key to your freedom is in your hands,' a man with a megaphone says, walking through the hallway that separates the two rows of cells.

'We will still win without you. All we want is to give the smart ones among you an opportunity to help themselves and their families.'

He tells us how people who cooperated and provided crucial information have gotten their freedom. There are thirty-five of us in a room the size of my office in the mosque.

Sale is thrown into my cell. His face is swollen and his mouth is bleeding. He nods at me.

'Where did they pick you up?' I ask him.

He hesitates and then says: 'At the mosque.'

'What were you doing there? You know we were all running away after they started arresting people.'

He is silent.

He tells me how there is now a twenty-four-hour curfew in the state because of people everywhere on the streets protesting the heavy hand of the soldiers. That they have ransacked my office in the mosque and all the rooms and even the school. That they met resistance at the school because our boys refused to let them in. After shooting a few of them the soldiers demolished one part of the fence and broke into Sheikh's offices.

'What of Malam Abduljalal?' I ask.

'He tried to reach out to Alhaji Usman. But Alhaji Usman refused to get involved. He said we should all allow the soldiers do their work. They have already arrested the local government chairman for being one of the people giving the Mujahideen money.'

Politicians are all the same. Now that Sheikh is dead, Alhaji Usman doesn't see any need to protect the movement. He is more interested in winning the elections.

A boy keeps screaming, 'I am not a Mujahideen,' in the cell opposite ours. They have still not given us any food or water.

I have just dozed off when they open the cell and throw in two men. One of them has been shot in both legs and the other's head is swollen and bleeding. I look again and the man with the swollen head is Mohammed Sani, the new Dariqa malam.

Day Three

Silence comes on the third day. The boy opposite is no longer screaming. Mohammed Sani is lying on his side, no longer breathing. There are no more whispers between the detainees. Our stomachs growl and rumble. The body of a man they brought in on the first day has started to swell and smell. I feel my body turning on me today. It feels like my stomach is eating and attacking itself.

The man with the megaphone passes by our cell and someone sitting by my side calls out to him.

'I want to talk.'

'OK. Talk,' the megaphone man says.

'Not here. Take me out.'

'You are sure you don't want to waste my time?'

'No sir, I have information.'

'Why did you not say so all this time that we have been asking.'

'I was afraid, sir.'

'Afraid of what?'

'Please sir, just get me out and I will tell you everything I know.'

'And how do you know what you know?'

'Please sir,' the man starts to cry.

'How do you know what you know?'

'I was in the Mujahideen enclave!' he screams.

'OK,' the megaphone man says, 'I am coming.'

The man moves away from the rest of us as if he is scared that we will attack him. 'Hypocrite,' an old man says and spits in his direction.

'Who likes the Mujahideen?' the old man continues. 'No one. But these people hate us equally. They don't care who is Mujahideen or Dariqa or Izala or Shiite. All they want is to oppress and kill Muslims.'

The man who wants to confess is breathing hard.

'Maybe you like it here, but I don't. Let my children judge me. And you are not Allah. Let Allah judge us for our actions. But I will rather be alive to take care of my family than dead trying to be stubborn.'

'Yes, because we here have no children or families ko?' the old man responds.

'Do what you will, but let me be and let Allah judge us all.'

The megaphone man comes back with three soldiers and leads the man away.

In the evening the soldiers return. Flashing a large torch light on our faces, they pick a skinny man and begin to take off his trousers. He kicks and screams and bites one of the soldiers. After one shot in the chest, he stops kicking and they strip him naked. With the light they examine the man's body.

'Look at it,' the one holding the torch says, pointing at the dead man's right thigh.

'Bastard! He is one of them. He has the mark.'

They start taking off everyone's trousers and separating people into groups. Those with a scar shaped like a crescent on the outer part of the right thigh and those without. They move Sale to the group of two men with scars. He looks up at me and then looks down. If anyone had told me that Sale was a Mujahideen, I would have said it was a lie but I might have understood. But a part of the Mujahideen killer squad? I wonder when he joined or if he had always been with them while he had access to the mosque and to all our documents. I want to spit on him as they march them all out of the cell. They make two of the men carry out the dead bodies.

Day Four

My eyes are blurry and I need to focus hard before I can make out any object. Sheikh appears. Then Jibril appears. Then Umma. Umma appears on my left and Aisha on my right. Umma is silent. Aisha is saying I should make up a story so that I leave this prison. I wish I had something to tell the megaphone man.

They bring in a large bowl of water that smells like it was used to wash fish and several plates of dry beans.

Most of us have our hands bound with either wire or handcuffs so people knock heads and slam their bodies against each other. The soldiers stand and watch and laugh. I refuse to join the struggle.

'You are too big for our beans ko?' one of the soldiers says to me, sniggering.

The old man who insulted the confessor yesterday was one of the first to grab a plate of food. He brings me a handful of beans. I shake my head.

'Don't be stupid, you will die if you do not eat,' he says.

'Thank you,' I say.

He gives it to the man to his right, who didn't get anything to eat. The man eats it out of his hand then crawls to the bowl of water and dips his head inside to drink.

'You, I know you,' the old man whispers, 'you are Sheikh Jamal's boy.'

I smile and nod gently.

'My name is Samaila. I sell fried fish at the junction in front of the house where Abdul-Nur used to live.'

My ears shut down and I cannot hear him anymore. I am hearing Jibril say English words to me and laughing when I don't pronounce them right. I am hearing him say Arabic words and hearing myself laugh when he doesn't pronounce them right.

Day Five

By nightfall almost everyone in our cell has a running stomach and is throwing up. It looks like cholera. Samaila throws up just close to my feet. He has been stooling all afternoon. Now he is too weak to even move. At some point he stretches out his hand to me.

'Boy,' he whispers.

'Samaila,' I reply.

Day Six

The soldiers bring in four of the prisoners from another cell to clear out more bodies from our cell. There are fifteen of us left and three of them are very sick. They move those of us who aren't stooling and vomiting to a tiny cell at the end of the hallway.

'I want paper,' I tell the soldier leading us away, 'paper and a pen or pencil.'

'To do what with?'

'Please I want something to write with.'

'Do you even know how to read? Is it not you people who are calling school a sin?'

'Please, just a paper and pen.'

'Shut up and move!'

'Please.'

'Look, if you talk to me again I will shoot you.'

Today they bring us bread and I know that I have to eat it. I close my eyes and hear the old man's voice in my ear. I hate him now for telling me his name. Without a name, it is easier to forget. The mind is a crazy thing. The things you want to keep forever fade away and the things you want to fade away stick like cashew stains on clothes.

The image of Sheikh's body flashes and disappears from time to time like a heartbeat. I want to remember him whole, not like that.

They have taken off our handcuffs. I think they need them for new, stronger prisoners.

One of the detainees tries to talk to me. I refuse to look at his face. I refuse to have another dead person stuck in my head.

I wish I could write.

Day Ten

The megaphone man has stopped coming. I can recite what he says word for word. It is confusing how I can miss him.

The man who has been bringing food regularly for the past two days, who even brought food twice yesterday and looks at me every time he does, is here again. He knows my name.

'Get up Ahmad. Let us go to my office.'

I am suspicious.

'I want to help you,' he adds as he takes me out of the cramped cell.

'Thank you,' I say.

'You see, the president is now interested in this our crisis and has asked us to do everything necessary to end it. I am from Sokoto myself. I don't like seeing our people in here. It makes me cry at night.'

He holds me by the shoulders as we take many turns away from the blocks of cells. My bones hurt so bad.

'You have been associated with Malam Abdul-Nur before, no?'

He drags a chair in a dimly lit room that smells like an abattoir and asks me to sit. There are three other men in the room.

'He used to be in our mosque before he left.'

'And?'

'After he left for Saudi Arabia, I never saw him again.'

'OK. But did you see any of his people?'

'No.'

'Are you sure about this? You see, I have been kind to you. It will be kind of you to make my job easier. In fact, I am thinking of moving you to a bigger cell where you will have water for ablution and everything.'

'I swear sir, I do not know any Mujahideen.'

'OK.'

He steps aside and nods to one of the men who ties my torso and legs to the chair I am sitting in, lifts me to a pillar in the room and ties my arms around the pillar. Then he is handed a pair of pliers. I am staring at the pliers. My head is telling me that it is all a joke and he will untie me and we will all laugh about this. My eyes become blurry and it makes the pliers look like a play object so that I start to believe my head about the joke. He whips out my phone from his pocket.

'I don't know why you are lying to me. These text messages were sent to you from that camp. I just want to make sure and give you an opportunity to cooperate with us before we go in and clear them out of there. I am disappointed in you. I will give you another opportunity to talk. But you must first learn the importance of telling the truth.'

He reaches for my nails. At first I don't feel anything because my head is still stuck in the belief that this is all a joke. Then the pain comes gushing. I feel it everywhere; in my nose and in my scrotum.

As blood flows down my arms, I scream until there are no more sounds coming from my stomach. The shock of the pain shuts me down and after a few minutes all I can hear are bubbly echoes.

There is pain. And there is pain.

Day Fourteen

If you stare at a wall hard enough, you begin to see patterns. Your mind connects the stains on the walls to make a face, an animal, a letter or an object. When I shut my eyes and look again, the pattern changes.

Jibril's face appears on a large part of the wall. I do not want to see his face. I shut my eyes and inhale deeply. He is safe and far away from all this madness and happy. And I must forget his face. I must forget his face.

I open my eyes and stare at a smaller portion of the wall. There is something shaped like a small microphone. I miss the call to prayer. These days I want to whisper it, say 'Allahu Akbar,' but it gets harder and harder as I wonder why we spend hours and hours saying that Allah is great when He abandons us in our time of need.

Does He abandon us?

Astaghfirullah.

Astaghfirullah.

Day Eighteen

The man with the pliers is here again.

You cannot prepare for pain. You cannot get used to it.

I have nothing to say to the man. I can only faint, again.

Day X

The only comfort of this cell is that it is not as hot as the others. The darkness here is complete, not decreasing or increasing. I started out guessing what time of the day it was by the temperature but these fevers keep me cold all the time. And finally I have stopped counting the days. Once in a while, they dump a few people in the cell. I never say a word to them. And they never last very long. They do not

understand that screaming or crying or jumping around trying to find a way to escape only wears you out. Especially
when the food is not regular and the guards take turns torturing you.

It is always A Mutu who brings them in.

'Landlord, I have brought you new tenants,' he says when
he throws in new people.

Once he came in and dragged me out along with other
bodies. They loaded me onto a truck, thinking I had died.
That was the one time I saw daylight. I was too dizzy to see
anything around.

'We have one still alive here o,' A Mutu shouted as he
climbed onto the back of the truck.

'Then help him with his journey,' someone replied from
the front. 'We really need to get going.'

'He does not need my help to die, it is not like he would
last long anyway.'

'In the name of God, please, finish him off and let's get
going.'

'Finish him off yourself, I am tired of killing these people.
This is not the job I was trained to do.'

'You are a weak man, I don't know how you became a
soldier.'

'Whatever.'

'OK then, A Mutu, take him back to the cell. Who gave
this weak man such a bold name, I do not know.'

'My boldness is in battle and not in killing half-dead
men.'

As he dragged me by my feet off the truck, I muttered:
'What date is it?'

'Shut up and die,' he said.

* * *

A Mutu flashes a light on me and then on the others he
brought recently. He picks me up by the arm and leads me
out of the cell. In another room, not as dark as my cell, he
asks me to sit. There is a plate of rice and beans and a big
plastic cup full of water.

'Eat,' he says and walks out of the room.

I drink the water first, finishing it quickly. I start to eat
with my hands before I notice a small plastic spoon beside
the plate. I continue eating with my hands. Swallowing hurts
my throat and as the food reaches my stomach I feel a sharp
biting pain and then I feel like throwing up. I stop for a while
holding my stomach and my hand over my mouth, thinking
I will lose everything I have eaten, but the muscles of my
stomach are too weak to bring up anything. A man walks in.
I cannot see his face.

'What is your name?' he asks, his voice an echo in my ear.

'Ahmad,' I reply.

'Do you like the food?'

I nod. My vision is getting less blurry.

'My name is Mohammed Abbas,' he says, 'and I am trying
to see if we can get you out of this place. I just need some
information from you and then we can start processing your
exit from here. I take it you are familiar with Malam Abdul-
Nur, the leader of the Mujahideen?'

I shake my head.

'No?' he asks.

'I used to know him, but it has been some time since he
r movement and since then I have not been in contact
n at all.'

'Are you sure about this?'

'By Allah, I swear it.'

'What if I tell you that people of your movement are also in the Mujahideen? I have even spoken with some of them, like Sale, for example. You know Sale, no?'

'Yes but I did not know that he was a Mujahideen. I only found out when they took him away from our cell.'

'But he mentioned your name. Are you saying that he is lying?'

'Of course he is lying.'

'I would have loved Sale to be here so you could say it to his face, but unfortunately he took ill and passed on a few days ago. Apparently he had stomach issues. Did you know he had stomach issues?'

'No.'

'And somehow I am tempted to believe Sale because he led us right to where Malam Abdul-Nur was hiding.'

'I swear I am not a Mujahideen,' I cry.

'No need to get upset, no need to get upset. Malam Abdul-Nur said the same thing when we got him the second time. He had shaved his beard and was pretending to be a cattle herder. You know it's funny he used the same words: "I swear I am not a Mujahideen." And then when we brought him in, he tried to attack my men. He didn't even give me the opportunity to have a chat with him like I am having a chat with you now, and that is sad because everyone deserves to be heard. Everyone deserves forgiveness.'

'So he is dead then?'

'Well, that was purely his choice, and the destiny of Allah.'

'Everything is over then?'

'Sale, before Allah took him,' he continues, ignoring my question, 'told us about your bosom friend, who is undoubtedly a Mujahideen.'

'Jibril is not a Mujahideen,' I shout.

'Oh, I see you are very acquainted with the person I am referring to. That means you can help me and I can help you. So now, let us put an end to all of this. I am sure you have been here too long. If you could just tell me where you think Jibril might be, we can all go home and see our loved ones.'

I want to tell him about our conversations, about how Jibril's heart was broken but his spirit was strong. But this man does not deserve the truth.

'Jibril is not a Mujahideen, that is all I know. You can beat me from now until tomorrow, refuse to give me food, but that is all I will tell you.' I push the plate aside and spread my palms on the table to show him I have no more nails for him to take.

The man gets up and tells A Mutu to take me away.

'To the pit!' he says.

PART FIVE

Black Spirit

Every time A Mutu comes to check for dead bodies he shouts 'Black Spirit!' to see if I am alive and I shuffle my feet to respond. I cannot say now how long I have been here. It feels like a really long time since he pulled out the last three bodies, since they last brought someone in. I don't know. Time plays tricks on me. I whisper words to myself—things I remember from my book, or from *Baba of Karo*, to stop my head from imploding, to remind myself I am still alive.

Before they throw you into the pit they tie a rope around your legs so that they can use a long hook to pull you out when you are dead.

It used to be that death was the worst thing that could happen to me. Then it was torture. Especially the pliers and screwdrivers. After ten fingers and ten toes, and you don't say anything, even the person torturing you knows there is nothing you can give them and they stop. They leave you to die. This is the hardest part. When the pain doesn't succeed. The period when they think the hunger will kill you and they leave you down here and there is nothing to show whether it is morning or night or afternoon. It is not the pain when you throw up bitter warm liquid because there is nothing to throw up and your body is turning on itself. It is not the spasms of your stomach when even the bitter liquid won't come up and your mouth is dry and cracked and your lips start to bleed when you try to open them. It is having no one to talk to and sleep deserting you and leaving you to experience every infinite moment of solitude. To count those moments, endlessly.

I wish A Mutu didn't throw the bread he throws in here, once in a while. It prolongs the suffering. The food beats my body into survival. And survival here is worse than being beaten.

It is interesting how time is different to different people. The soldiers care very much what hour of the day it is. They say things like nine hundred hours and fourteen hundred hours. It must make time drag to count every hour of every day. I can understand the useful things, like sunrise and sunset and midday; when it is time to pray and when it is time to break one's fast. And what really is an hour? I am not sure that anyone can say for certain what an hour is. Because my hours are definitely longer than the hours of the soldiers outside, who can go home and lie on soft beds. As some hours are short, so others are long. Or maybe I am having a problem separating what is real from what just happens in my head. I don't even know any more if what happens in my head is not real. Because I think of things like anger or pain when someone offends you. If you do not know of the thing that was done, it does not offend you. But as soon as you find out, something grows in your head and in your heart and in your body where once there was calm and peace and it is called anger or pain. And sometimes when that person apologises genuinely, you can feel that anger melt away like ice in the heat. So, what makes one thought or feeling real and another unreal. What makes time move differently for me at different times?

Sometimes it feels like I am going crazy and I have to speak to myself loudly, to convince myself I am still here, alive. Memory feels like a curse but it is the only thing that keeps me sane. In my mind I am a child again, sitting on Malam Junaidu's cracked concrete floor, reciting the words of the Quran. The kuka tree in Bayan Layi stands tall and alone and the boys of Bayan Layi send cigarette and wee-wee smoke up into the air. I see myself, blowing wee-wee smoke, feeling invincible and wanting to fly. I see the ashes form after we drag, turning leaves into smoke and powder, like life. My life. Every day feels like a drag that brings me closer to being burnt out, turned to ash. These days I don't know which of my memories are real and which ones are dreams, made up in my mind to keep me from shutting down. I wonder if Allah is sometimes like me, who doesn't always have a why; whether He just does things or allows things to happen because He can. Or if he always has a why, a plan, a reason for all this suffering. Today if Allah will hear me, before I die here I want him to give me a person who will write down my story like the woman who wrote that of Baba of Karo. I think it is a nice thing that long after you die people can get to read the stories of your life. The only problem is, Baba of Karo knew everything about her relatives. What do I know about my brothers and my uncles and my aunts, apart from Khadija and Shuaibu, whom I do not even know very well. But Sheikh, I can tell a hundred pages about him. As I can about Jibril. Is family really family if your relatives are strangers to you? Are they not blood, those for whom you would risk your life and die; those who know how your heart beats, and what makes you laugh and what makes you cry; those whose secrets are your secrets?

'This one refuses to die o,' A Mutu says, 'we call him Black Spirit.'

The man standing with A Mutu peeps into the narrow pit. Someone is shining a torch behind them. I can only see his square head and high, stiff collar. I drag myself into an upright position and squint. 'Please,' I want to shout out to them. But I have pleaded until my mouth, knowing how useless the word is, has prevented me from voicing it. Pleas have no value in this pit. Only dying can stop them from doing what they want.

'Where did you find him?' the man with the square head asks.

'Sokoto,' A Mutu replies.

'Before or after the elections?'

'Before, sir. He is getting to nine months now.'

'Take him back where you picked him up.'

'Sir?'

'Are you deaf? I say take him back. I want this place empty!'

'Yes, sir!'

A Mutu lowers a hook and pulls me up by the legs so that I am upside down. I am dizzy. When I am out, he puts a khaki bag over my entire head. It smells of sweat and blood. He hums the one song that has been on his lips since I came here. When he sings 'We are saying thank you Jesus, thank you Jesus, thank youuuu Laaaw-ooord . . .' I want to ask him if he knows any other song. I don't know why he keeps thanking Jesus when he comes around. He holds me by the arm and I feel my feet leave the ground, as if I was an empty bucket. He drops me gently at the back of the truck.

My bones hurt. For the first time in a long while, I smell something apart from decay. I inhale lightly. Dust. Dust smells like the best Arabian incenses now. I scratch the hair on my neck. The little light that filters through the khaki cloth over my head, more light than I have seen in the past many months, hurts my eyes. Someone climbs the back of the truck with me. I know him by smell. A Mutu smells of onions fried in stale palm oil.

After about an hour, I stop hearing any voices around and the truck begins to slow down. As the engine goes dead, I wait for the boots that will kick me off the truck. Maybe this is what the man meant by take him back. To take me somewhere and shoot me. This will be an act of kindness.

A Mutu grabs me gently by the arms and lifts me. He is careful, like he is afraid that my skin will peel off or my bones will snap. He leans me against a wall and makes me sit. Then he loosens the ropes around my legs.

I hear him walking away. I inhale and shut my eyes and wait for it, my relief. The engine starts and the truck begins to drive away. When I can no longer hear anything, I lift my hands and pull up the khaki mask. The light feels like needles in my eyes. I am in the shade outside a classroom in an empty school. There is no one else around. By my side is a sachet of water, a black polythene bag with rice in it and a pair of old slippers. Everything is grey and blurry beyond a few meters.

Away from the school, I stop by a car, supporting my weight on a stick I picked up in one of the classrooms. At first it looks like someone is looking back at me, but there is no one in the car. I touch my face. I do not know this old, shrivelled person whose eyes look like that of a rabid dog. They should have just shot me.

There are more soldiers than civilians on the streets. At every checkpoint there are metal drums and sandbags and huge rocks on the road to make cars drive slowly in a zigzag way. Even the checkpoint in front of the police station is manned by soldiers. The cars, the bicycles, the people and even the animals all seem to be moving very fast; everyone seems to be in a hurry.

All over the partly demolished fence of our school is the phrase NO MORE HAQIQIY. Most of them have HAQIQIY cancelled out and replaced with MUJAHIDEEN. When people pass by soldiers, they have to raise their hands in the air. People carrying big bags are stopped and searched.

A soldier stares at me. I try to stand upright but my back feels like it is about to break. He points his gun at me. I stop trying to put my hands in the air and I look him in the eye willing him to pull the trigger. He walks towards me pointing the gun at my chest and motions to me to keep moving. He looks just like a child wearing an oversized uniform. There is fear in his eyes. I spit on the floor and drag myself away.

On the floor there is a half-eaten sugarcane. I pick it up. It still tastes sweet but it is dry and dusty. I put it in my pocket.

Our mosque has been almost completely demolished. The motor park is full of soldiers and most of the shops around it are closed. Chuks' medicine store now has a woman selling provisions and travelling bags. I don't know any of the drivers. The only person I can recognise is Saudatu who is still selling kosai and koko here. I call out her name.

'What do you want?' she asks.

'Do you not know me?'

'I do not know you, mister. If you are not going to buy anything please move away for others who want to buy.'

'Why are you speaking to him like this? If you do not recognise him, just say so,' a middle-aged man standing behind me says to her.

As I turn around, she asks me who I am.

My mouth feels paralysed. I am unable to speak for a few seconds. Finally, when my lips come free, I say, 'Black Spirit.'

'You see? He is a madman.' Saudatu says to the man.

On my way out of the motor park I see a sticker on a pillar:

ALHAJI SENATOR USMAN MAMMAN DAHIRU
WEDS
AISHATU

The two people on it are smiling, both baring gold teeth from Mecca.

'My wife,' I say to the two men sitting on a bench just by the sticker. One of them gets up to see what I am pointing at.

'My wife,' I repeat, 'she is my wife.' He hisses when he sees the picture and walks away.

The soldiers. It is the soldiers who are making everyone so aggressive.

I walk in through the open gate in my old compound. In the gate house a small radio sits on the window sill playing loud Hausa music. A chair with one broken back leg leans against the wall. There are old clothes scattered on an old mat. No one around. I walk slowly towards the room I once called home. The door is broken down and there are books and papers lying everywhere. Huge brown cloud patterns cover the ceiling and some of the ceiling boards sag. The roof has leaked. I wish now that I had hid my notebook somewhere in the room. When I close my eyes I can see the lines on the page, the words.

I can hear the radio in the gate house from the room. The news is being read in Hausa. A newscaster is talking about a suicide bombing and I am shocked to hear it is here in Nigeria. This is not what I want to hear now. I block the newscaster's voice out of my head and look around the room. I cannot stop asking myself why they let me go, why they did not kill me. Perhaps someone told them I was innocent. Perhaps they just got tired of keeping me. Or maybe, like with many things in the world, there is no why and I should stop thinking things that only make my head hurt. Allah knows.

Inside the wardrobe, I see my old wooden chasbi. I pick it up and slowly roll the beads in my fingers.

Subhannallah . . .

Alhamdillillah . . .

Allahu Akbar . . .

In charcoal, at the bottom right corner on the wall opposite the door, there are words in tiny scribbles:

I came back for you. They said you were dead but I didn't believe. I will come back again, insha Allah.

He does not write his name. He knows I will know.

I am lightheaded. I heave a sigh. My heart tells me he is OK. Jibril is OK. I stretch out on the cool concrete floor. Time slows down again. I think of all the things I must do: cut my hair, wash with hot water, start writing out my story. Then take a bus and go wherever it is headed.

Acknowledgments

Basiru, the almajiri from Sokoto I met in Zaria, whose story made me create Dantala, who will probably never read this book; Miriam Kotzin at Per Contra, who first gave 'Bayan Layi' life; The Caine Prize for African Writing, whose shortlisting of Bayan Layi encouraged me to take the story further; Azan John, who would have been proud of this book, as he was of everything I ever wrote, who lives forever in me; Chika Unigwe, my sister, friend and mentor who has her hand in every story of mine; Jeremy Weate who first forced the manuscript out of my hands and believed in it, before I did; Bibi Bakare-Yusuf who gave this child of mine a home and keeps being my biggest supporter; Mirella Mahlstein, my fsbdp, who patiently stood with me until I finished, who endured my moments of frustration and irritation, who was my anchor on those down days; Toby Mundy, my diligent agent, who makes his very difficult job look so easy; Steffi Hirsbrunner, my dear friend and a great promoter of my work, who makes sure I always have a home and family in Berlin; Abubakar Adam Ibrahim, my braza, my friend, my travelling companion, my Arabic 'consultant,' the sober one; The Civitella Ranieri Fellowship where I put finishing touches to this book, for the gifts of time and space; Steve Devitt, my grumpy old friend, who read my work and forced me on his students, who believed in me, whose weekly emails give me life; the thorough Kate Haines who saw things I could not see; the diligent Allison Malecha at Grove Atlantic who had to deal with my constant emails; Quiterie de Roquefeuil with whom I had many fights over this story, who sometimes knew and cared about the characters more than I did; Carmen McCain!

Eugenia Abu, for the amazing support. Always.

Emma Shercliff, Umma Aliyu, Hadiza Ibrahim Halid, Jude Dibia, Femke van Zeijl, The Ebedi Residency, Faith Adiele, Nkem Ivara, Anthony Ivara, Ngozi Oti, Zakari Usman Mijinyawa, Jazzmine Breary, Usho Smith Adawa, Friday John Aba, ANA Kaduna, Emman Shehu, Cassava Republic.

Dad, mum, Jummai, David,
Thank you.